"What a ~~...~~ different for this church? For this town?"

He paused, not knowing how to respond. "I just think we need to pick our battles, Tangie. Some mountains aren't worth dying on."

She stared at him, her big brown eyes screaming out her frustration. "We both need to go home and sleep on this," she suggested. "I'm too tired to make much sense out of things tonight. And besides, we're meeting tomorrow afternoon at the church to finalize things, right? Let's just drop it for now."

"But I don't want to leave it hanging in midair till then." Gregg shook his head. "I want to understand why you're being so stubborn about this. What are you thinking, anyway?"

"I'm thinking this will be a good time to teach Margaret a couple of life lessons. The top dog doesn't always get the bone, Gregg."

"She's a kid, not a golden retriever," he responded.

Back and forth they went, arguing about who should—or shouldn't—play the various roles in the play. All the while, Gregg felt more and more foolish about the words coming out of his mouth. In fact, at one point, he found himself unable to focus on anything other than the pain on her beautiful face and guilt over the fact that he'd put it there.

Tangie's hands began to tremble—likely from the anger— and he reached to take them, suddenly very ashamed of himself for getting her so worked up.

With hands clasped, she stared at him, silence rising up between them. Except for the sound of Gregg's heartbeat, which he imagined she must be able to hear as clearly as he did, everything grew silent.

Then, like a man possessed, Gregg did the unthinkable.

He kissed her.

JANICE HANNA (also known as Janice A. Thompson) has published over thirty books for the Christian market, most lighthearted and/or wedding themed. Working with quirky characters and story ideas suits this fun-loving author. She particularly enjoys contemporary romantic comedies. Wedding-themed books come naturally to Janice, since she's coordinated nearly a dozen weddings, including recent ceremonies/receptions for all four daughters. Most of all, she loves sharing her faith with readers and hopes they will catch a glimpse of the real "happily ever after" in her stories.

Books by Janice A. Thompson

HEARTSONG PRESENTS

Books by Janice Hanna

Don't miss out on any of our super romances. Write to us at the following address for information on our newest releases and club information.

Heartsong Presents Readers' Service
PO Box 721
Uhrichsville, OH 44683

Or visit www.heartsongpresents.com

Sweet Harmony

Janice Hanna

Heartsong Presents

In loving memory of one of my dearest drama buddies of all time, Robin Tompkins, currently performing on the greatest stage of all.

A note from the Author:
I love to hear from my readers! You may correspond with me by writing:

Janice Hanna
Author Relations
PO Box 721
Uhrichsville, OH 44683

ISBN 978-1-60260-557-2

SWEET HARMONY

All scripture quotations, unless otherwise indicated, are taken from the HOLY BIBLE, NEW INTERNATIONAL VERSION®. NIV®. Copyright © 1973, 1978, 1984 by International Bible Society. Used by permission of Zondervan. All rights reserved.

All of the characters and events in this book are fictitious. Any resemblance to actual persons, living or dead, or to actual events is purely coincidental.

Our mission is to publish and distribute inspirational products offering exceptional value and biblical encouragement to the masses.

PRINTED IN THE U.S.A.

one

"Life is better in Harmony. If you don't believe me, come on up here and see for yourself."

Tangie laughed as she heard her grandmother's cheerful words. Leaning back against the pillows, she shifted the cell phone to her other ear and tried to imagine what her life would be like if she actually lived in her grandparents' tiny hometown of Harmony, New Jersey. "Thanks, Gran-Gran, but I'm no small-town girl," she said, finally. "I've spent the last four years in New York, remember?"

"How could I forget?" Her grandmother's girlish laugh rippled across the telephone line. "I've told every person I know that my granddaughter is a Broadway star. . .that she knows all of the big names in the Big Apple."

Tangie groaned. "I might know a few people, but I'm no star, trust me." In fact, these days she couldn't even seem to find a long-term acting gig, no matter how far off-Broadway she auditioned. So, on Christmas Eve she'd packed her bags and headed home to Atlantic City. Tangie had spent much of the drive praying, asking God what she should do. His silence had been deafening.

Now Christmas had passed and a new year approached. Still, Tangie felt no desire to return to the Big Apple. Safely tucked into the same bed she'd slept in every night as a little girl, she just wanted to stay put. Possibly forever. And maybe that was for the best. She'd felt for some time that things were winding down, career-wise. Besides, she'd seen more than enough drama over the past four years. . .and not just on the stage. So what if her days on the stage were behind her? Maybe—in spite of her best efforts—she wasn't destined to perform on Broadway.

"I'm telling you, Harmony is the perfect place for you." Gran-Gran's words interrupted her thoughts. "You need a break from big-city life. It's peaceful here, and the scenery is breathtaking, especially during the holidays. It'll do you good. And it'll do my heart good to have you. I'm sure Gramps would agree."

"Oh, you don't have to win me over on the beauty of upstate New Jersey," Tangie assured her. She'd visited her mom's parents enough to know that Harmony was one of the prettiest places on planet Earth, especially in the wintertime when the snows left everything a shimmering white. Pausing a moment, she thought about her options. "Might sound silly, but my first reaction is to just stay here."

"In Atlantic City?" her grandmother asked, the surprise in her voice evident. "Would you work at the candy shop? I thought you'd given up on that idea years ago when you headed to New York."

"Yeah." Tangie sighed as she shifted her position in the bed to get more comfortable. "But Mom and Dad are about to head out in their RV again, so Taffie's bound to need my help, especially with the new baby."

Tangie couldn't help but smile as she reflected on her older sister's mothering skills. Baby Callie had lovely brown tufts of hair and kissable apple dumpling cheeks. And her big brown eyes melted Tangie's heart every time.

Yes, it might be nice to stay home for a change. Settle in. Hang out at the candy shop with people who loved her. People who would offer encouragement and help her forget about the thousand ways she'd failed over the past few years, not just professionally, but personally, as well. All of the parts she'd auditioned for but hadn't received. All of the plays she'd been in that had closed unexpectedly. All of the would-be relationships that had ended badly.

Tangie sighed.

"Let me tell you the real reason for my call." The determination in her grandmother's voice grew by the minute. "No point in beating around the bush. Our church is looking for a drama director for the kids' ministry. I suggested you and the pastor jumped on the idea."

"W—what?"

"There's nothing wrong with your hearing, honey. Harmony might be small, but the church certainly isn't. It's grown by leaps and bounds since you were here last, and the children's ministry is splitting at the seams. Our music pastor has been trying to involve the kids in his productions, but he doesn't know the first thing about putting on a show. Not the acting part, anyway. We need a real drama director. Someone skilled at her craft. . .who knows what she's doing."

"Why hire one?" Tangie asked. "Why not just find someone inside the church with those talents and abilities?"

"No one has your qualifications," Gran-Gran stated. "You know everything about set design, staging, costumes, and acting. You're a wealth of knowledge. And you've worked on Broadway, for heaven's sake. Gregg doesn't mind admitting he knows very little about putting on shows. He attempted one with the kids last week. A Christmas production. But it was, well—"

"Wait. Who's Gregg?" Tangie interrupted.

"Gregg. Our music pastor. The one I was just talking about. You remember him, right?"

"Hmm." Tangie paused to think about it. "Yeah, I think I remember him. Sort of a geeky looking guy? Short hair. Looks like his mother dressed him?"

Gran-Gran clucked her tongue. "Tangie, shame on you. He's a wonderful, godly man. Very well groomed. And tidy."

Tangie looked at the mess in her bedroom and chuckled. "Sounds like my dream guy."

"Well, don't laugh. There are reams of young women trying to catch his eye. Good thing they don't all see things the way you do. Besides, half the women in our Prime Timers class are praying for a wife for Gregg, so it's just a matter of time before God parts the Red Sea and brings the perfect woman his way."

"Mm-hmm. But let's go back to talking about that show he put on. What happened?"

"It was terrible." Gran-Gran sighed. "And I don't just mean terrible. It was awful. Embarrassing, actually. The kids didn't memorize any of their lines, and their costumes—if you could call them that—looked more like bathrobes. And don't even get me started on the set. He built it out of cardboard boxes he found behind our local hardware store. You could still see the Home Depot logo through the paint."

"Ugh. Give me a break." Sounded pretty amateurish. Then again, she'd been in some productions over the years that weren't exactly stellar. . .in any sense of the word, so who was she to pass judgment?

"The music part was great," Gran-Gran said. "That's Gregg's real gift. He knows music. But the acting part was painful to watch. If my best friend's grandkids hadn't been in it, Gramps and I probably would've left during the intermission."

"I've seen a few shows like that," Tangie said. She chuckled, and then added, "I've *been* in a few shows like that."

Her grandmother laughed. "Honey, with you *everything's* a show. And that's exactly why I think you'd be perfect for this. Ever since you graduated from acting school last spring, you've been trying to find out where you belong. Right?"

"Right." Tangie sighed.

"And didn't you tell me you worked with a children's group at the theater school?"

"Yes. I directed a couple of shows with them. They were great." In fact, if she admitted the truth to herself, working with the kids had been one of the few things she'd really felt good about.

"Think of all the fun you'll have working with the children at church, then," Gran-Gran said. "You'll be able to share both your love of acting and the love of the Lord."

"True. I was really limited at the school." The idea of working in a Christian environment sounded good. Really good, in fact.

"They need someone with your experience and your zeal. I've never known anyone with as much God-given talent and ability, and so creative, too. Gregg is pretty much 'in the box.' And you, well. . ." Her grandmother's voice trailed off.

"Say no more." Tangie laughed. She'd busted out of the box years ago when she dyed her spiky hair bright orange and got that first tattoo. Glancing down at her Tweety Bird pajamas and fuzzy slippers, she had to wonder what the fine folks of Harmony, New Jersey, would think of such an "out of the box" kind of girl.

Only one way to know for sure. Maybe it would be best to start the new year in a new place, after all.

Tangie drew in a deep breath, then spurted her impromptu answer. "Gran-Gran, tell them I accept. Look for me tomorrow afternoon. Tangie Carini is coming to Harmony!"

❧

Gregg Burke left the staff meeting at Harmony Community Church, his thoughts tumbling around in his head. He climbed into his car and pointed it toward home—the tiny wood-framed house on the outskirts of town. With the flip of a switch, the CD player kicked on. Gregg continued to press the FORWARD button until he located the perfect song—a worship tune he'd grown to love.

Ah. Perfect.

He leaned back against the seat and shifted his SUV into DRIVE. As he pulled out onto the winding country road, Gregg reflected on the meeting he'd just attended. The church was growing like wildfire; that was a fact. And while he understood the need to keep up with the times, he didn't want to jump onboard every trend that came along. He'd seen other churches pull out the stops to become hip and trendy, and some of them had lost their original passion for the Word and for prayer. No way would he go along with that.

On the other hand, some folks had accused him of being set in his ways. Unwilling to bend. What was it the pastor had just said at the meeting? "Gregg, you're the oldest twenty-six-year-old I've ever known." Dave's words had pricked Gregg's heart. He didn't want others to see him as stiff or unbending.

Lord, am I? I don't want to get in the way of whatever You want to do, but I think we need to be careful here. I know we need to do everything we can to reach out to people. I'm all about that. I just pray we move carefully. Thoughtfully.

As Gregg maneuvered a sharp turn, a bank of snow on the side of the road caught his eye. Late December was alwa[y] such a beautiful time of year in Harmony, but this year h[e] looked forward to the change of seasons more than ever. Th[e] countless piles of snow would melt away into oblivion. Greg[g] could hardly wait for the warmth of spring. Gramps—hi[s] adopted grandfather—had already informed him there wer[e] at least ten or twenty trout in the lake with his name on them. He could hardly wait to reel them in.

On the other hand, the eventual change in seasons forced Gregg to think about something he'd rather *not* think about— the Easter production he'd just agreed to do with the children.

At once, his attitude shifted. While Gregg wanted to go along with Dave's idea of reaching out to the community, the suggestion of putting on three to four musical performances a year with the children concerned him. First, he didn't want to take that much time away from the adult choir. Those singers needed him. Second, he didn't work as well with kids as some people thought he did. In fact, he wasn't great with kids. . .at all.

"It's not that I don't like children," he said to himself. "They're just. . .different."

The ones he'd worked with in the Christmas play were rowdy, and they didn't always pay attention. And, unlike his adult choir members, the kids didn't harmonize very well, no matter how hard he worked with them. In fact, one or two of the boys couldn't carry a tune in a bucket. Why their parents had insisted they participate in the musical. . .

Stop it, Gregg.

He shook his head, frustrated with himself for thinking like that. Every child should have the opportunity to learn, to grow. How many chances had he been given as a kid? He'd struggled through softball, hockey, and a host of other sports before finally realizing singing was more his bag.

The more he thought about it, the worse he felt. How many of those boys, like himself, were without a father? He knew of at least one or two who needed a strong, positive male influence. Had the Lord orchestrated this whole plan to put him in that position, maybe? If so, did he have it in him?

"Father, help me. I don't want to blow this. But I guess it's obvious I'm going to need Your help more than ever. Remind me of what it was like to be a kid." He shivered, just thinking about it.

Gregg pulled the car onto the tiny side street, then crawled along the uneven road until he reached his driveway. His house sat back nearly a quarter mile, tucked away in the trees. At the end of the driveway, he stopped at the mailbox and snagged today's offering from the local mail carrier. Then he pulled his car into the garage, reached for his belongings, and headed inside.

Entering his home, Gregg hung his keys on the hook he'd placed strategically near the door and put his jacket away in the closet, being careful to fasten every snap. He placed the pile of mail on the kitchen counter, glanced through it, then organized it into appropriate categories: To be paid. To be tossed. To be pondered.

Oh, if only he could organize the kids with such ease. Then, perhaps, he wouldn't dread the days ahead.

two

Tangie made the drive from Atlantic City to Harmony in a little less than three hours. Though the back roads were slick—the winter in full swing—she managed to make it to her grandparents' house with little problem. In fact, the closer she got to Harmony, the prettier everything looked, especially with Christmas decorations still in place. Against the backdrop of white, the trees showcased their bare branches. Oh, but one day. . .one day the snows would melt and spring would burst through in all of its colorful radiance. Tangie lived for the springtime.

"Color, Lord," she whispered. "That's what gets me through the winter. The promise of color when the snows melt!"

As she pulled her car into the drive, a smile tugged at the edges of her lips. Little had changed at the Henderson homestead in the twenty-two years she'd been coming here. Oh, her grandfather had painted the exterior of the tiny wood-framed house a few years ago, shifting from a light tan to a darker tan. It had created quite a stir. But other than that, everything remained the same.

"Lord, I'm going to need Your strength. You know how I am. I'm used to the hustle and bustle of Times Square. Eating in crowded delis and listening to taxi cabs honk as they go tearing by. Racing from department store to theater. I'm not used to a quiet, slow-paced, solitary life. I—"

She didn't have time to finish her prayer. Gran-Gran stood at the front door, waving a dishtowel and hollering. Tangie climbed out of the car, and her grandmother sprinted her way across the snowy yard like a track star in the making. *Okay, so maybe not everything moves slowly here.*

"Oh, you beautiful thing!" Her grandmother giggled as she reached to touch Tangie's hair. "What have you done now?"

"Don't you like it? I thought red was a nice color with my skin tone."

"That's *red*?" Gran-Gran laughed. "If you say so. In the sunlight, I think I see a little purple in there."

"Probably. But that's okay, too. You know me, Gran-Gran. All things bright. . ."

"And beautiful," her grandmother finished. "I know, I know."

Tangie grabbed her laptop and overnight bag, leaving the other larger suitcases in the trunk.

Gran-Gran chattered all the way into the house. Once inside, she hollered, "Herbert, we've got a guest!"

"Oh, I'm no guest. Don't make a fuss over me." Tangie set her stuff on the nearest chair and looked around the familiar living room. The place still smelled the same—like a combination of cinnamon sticks and old books. But something else had changed. "Hey, you've moved the furniture."

"Yes." Gran-Gran practically beamed. "Do you like it?"

Tangie shrugged. "Sure. I guess so." To be honest, she felt a little odd with the room all turned around. It had always been the other way. *Whoa, girl. You've never cared about things staying the same before. Snap out of it! Let your grandmother live a little! Walk on the wild side!*

Seconds later, her grandfather entered the room. His gray hair had thinned even more since her last visit, and his stooped shoulders threw her a little. When had this happened?

"Get over here, Tangerine, and give your old Gramps a hug!" He opened his arms wide as he'd done so many times when she was a little girl.

Tangie groaned at the nickname, but flew into his arms nonetheless. Sure enough, he still smelled like peppermint and Old Spice. Nothing new there.

"How are your sisters?" he asked with a twinkle in his eye.

"Taffie's great. Motherhood suits her. And Candy. . ."

Tangie smiled, thinking of her middle sister. "Candy's still flying high."

"Loving her life as a pilot for Eastway, from what I hear." Gramps nodded. "That's my girl. A high-flying angel."

"And you!" Gran-Gran drew near and placed another kiss on her cheek. "You're straight off the stages of Broadway."

"More like off-off-Broadway." Tangie shrugged, determined to change the direction of the conversation. "I come bearing gifts!" She reached for the bag she and Taffie had carefully packed with candies from the family's shop on the boardwalk.

Gramps' eyes lit up as he saw the CARINI'S CONFECTIONS logo on the bag. "Oh, I hope you've got some licorice in there."

"I do. Three different flavors."

"And some banana taffy?" Gran-Gran asked.

"Naturally. You didn't think I'd forget, did you? I know it's your favorite."

Gramps tore into the licorice and popped a piece in his mouth. As he did, a look of pure satisfaction seemed to settle over him. "Mmm. I'm sure glad that daughter of mine married into the candy business. It's made for a pretty sweet life for the rest of us."

Tangie nodded. "Yeah, Mom was born for the sweet stuff. Only now she seems happier touring the country in that new RV she and dad bought last month."

"I heard they had a new one," Gran-Gran said. "Top of the line model."

"Yes, and they're going to travel the southern states to stay warm during the winter." Tangie couldn't help but smile as she reflected on the pictures Mom had sent from Florida awhile back. In one of them, her father was dressed in Bermuda shorts on bottom and a Santa costume on top. The caption read CONFUSED IN MIAMI.

"I've never understood the fascination with going from place to place in an RV," Gramps said, as he settled into his recliner and reached for another piece of licorice. "Who wants to live in a house on wheels when you've got a perfectly good house that sits still?" He gestured to his living room, and Tangie grinned.

"You've got a good point," she said as she reached for a piece of taffy. "But I think Mom was born with a case of wanderlust."

"Oh yes," Gran-Gran agreed. "That girl never could stay put when she was a little thing. Always flitting off here or there."

"I'm kind of the same way, I guess." Tangie shrugged. "An adventurer. And I do tend to flit from one thing to another." She sighed.

"Well, we hope you'll stay put in Harmony awhile," Gramps said, giving her a wink. "Settle in. Make some friends."

A mixture of emotions rushed over Tangie at her grandfather's words. While there was some appeal to long-lasting friendships, she wasn't the type to settle in. No, the past four years had proven that. Jumping from one thing to another—one show to another—seemed more her mode of operation. Was the Lord doing something different this time? Calling her to stay put for a while?

"Let's get you settled in your new room." Gran-Gran gestured toward the hallway. "Do you need Gramps to get your things?"

"Oh, I don't mind getting them myself."

"Not while I'm living and breathing!" Her grandfather, rising from the recliner, gave her a stern look. She tossed him her keys, then watched with a smile as he headed outdoors to fetch her bags.

Tangie traipsed along on her grandmother's heels until they reached the spare bedroom—the second room on the right past the living room. She'd slept in the large four-poster bed dozens of times over the years, of course, but never for more than a couple of nights at a stretch. Was this really her new room?

She smiled as she saw the porcelain dolls on the dresser and the hand-embroidered wall hangings. Not exactly her taste in decor, but she wouldn't complain. Unless she decided to stay long-term, of course. Then she would likely replace some of the wall hangings with the framed playbills from all of the shows she'd been in. Now that would really change the look of the room, wouldn't it!

Tangie spent the next several minutes putting away her clothes. The folded items went in the dresser. Gran-Gran had been good enough to empty the top three drawers. The rest of Tangie's things were hung in the already-crowded closet. Oh well. She'd make do. Likely this trek to the small town of Harmony wouldn't last long, anyway. Besides, she knew what it was like to live in small spaces. She and her roommate Marti had barely enough room to turn around in the five-hundred-square-foot apartment they'd shared in Manhattan. This place was huge in comparison.

As she wrapped up, Gran-Gran turned her way with a smile. "Let's get this show on the road, honey. Pastor Hampton is waiting for us at the church. He wants to meet you and give you your marching orders."

"A—already?" Tangie shook her head. "But I look awful. I'm still wearing my sweats, and my hair needs a good washing before I meet anyone." She pulled a compact out of her purse, groaning as she took a good look at herself. Her usually spiky hair looked more like a normal "do" today. And without a fresh washing, even the color of her hair looked less vibrant. . . more ordinary. Maybe freshening up her lipstick would help. She scrambled for the tube of Ever-Berry lip gloss.

"Oh, pooh." Gran-Gran waved her hand. "Don't worry about any of that. We've got to be at the church at three and it's a quarter till. If you're a good girl, I'll make some of that homemade hot chocolate you love so much when we get back."

"You've got it!" Tangie pressed the compact and lip gloss back into her purse—a beaded forties number she'd purchased at a resale shop on a whim.

Minutes later she found herself in the backseat of her grandparents' 1998 Crown Victoria, puttering and sputtering down the road.

"This thing's got over two hundred thousand miles on it," Gramps bragged, taking a sharp turn to the right. "Hope to put another hundred on it before one of us gives out."

"One of us?" Tangie's grandmother looked at him, stunned. "You mean you or me?"

"Well, technically, I meant me or the car." He grinned. "But I'm placing my bets on the car. She's gonna outlive us all."

"I wouldn't doubt it."

Gramps went off on a tangent about the car, but Gran-Gran seemed distracted. She turned to wave at an elderly neighbor shuffling through the snow, dressed in a heavy coat and hat. "Oh, look. There's Clarence, checking his mail. I need to ask him how Elizabeth's doing." She rolled down her window and hollered out, "Clarence!" The older man paused, mail in hand, and turned their way.

As the others chatted about hernias, rheumatism, and the need for warmer weather, Tangie pondered her choice to move here. *Lord, what have I done? If I've made an impulsive decision, help me unmake it. But if I'm supposed to be here. . .*

She never got any further in her prayer. Though it didn't make a lick of sense, somehow she just knew. . .she was supposed to be here.

⁂

Gregg worked against the clock in his office, transcribing music for the Sunday morning service. The musicians would be counting on him, as would the choir. As he wrapped up, he glanced at his watch and sighed. Three forty-five? Man. He still had to call Darla, the church's part-time pianist, full-time self-appointed matchmaker, to talk about that one tricky key change. She'd struggled with it at their last rehearsal.

Leaning back in his chair, Gregg reflected on a conversation he'd had with Dave earlier this morning. Looked like the church had decided to hire a drama director. Interesting. In some ways, he felt a little put off by the idea. Was he really so bad at directing shows that they needed to actually hire someone?

On the other hand, the notion of someone else helping out did offer some sense of relief. That way, he could focus on his own work. Work he actually enjoyed. Music was his respite. His sanctuary. He ran to it as others might run to sports or TV shows. Music energized him and gave him a sense of purpose. Daily, Gregg thanked the Lord for the sheer pleasure of earning a living doing the thing he loved most.

Now, if only he could figure out how to get around that whole "productions" thing, he'd be a happy, happy man.

At four thirty, he finished up his tasks and prepared to leave. His thoughts shifted to Ashley, the children's ministry leader. At Darla's prompting, Gregg had worked up the courage to ask Ashley out and she'd agreed. Wonder of wonders! Would tonight's dinner date at Gratzi's win her over? From what he'd been told, she loved Italian food. For that matter, he did, too. Still, a plate of fettuccine Alfredo didn't automatically guarantee true love. No, for that he'd have to think bigger. Maybe chicken parmesan.

Deep in thought, Gregg left his office. He walked down the narrow hallway, arms loaded with sheets of music. Just as he reached Dave's office, the door swung open and Gramps Henderson stepped out. The two men nearly collided. Gregg came to such an abrupt stop that his sheets of music went flying. He immediately dropped to his knees and began the task of organizing his papers.

"Let me help with that."

Gregg looked up into the eyes of a woman—maybe in her early twenties—with the oddest color hair he'd ever seen. He tried not to stare, but it was tough. He went back to the task at hand, snatching the papers. She worked alongside him, finally handing him the last page.

"Ooo, is that the contemporary version of the 'Hallelujah Chorus'?" she asked, gazing at him with soul-piercing intensity. For a second he found himself captivated by her dark brown eyes.

"Yes." He gave her an inquisitive look. How would she know that?

She flashed a warm smile, but he was distracted by all of the earrings. Well, that and the tiny sparkler in her nose. Was that a diamond? Very bizarre. He had to wonder if it ever bothered her. . .say, when she got a cold.

Gregg rose to his feet, then reached a hand to help the young woman up. By the time they were both standing, Mrs. Henderson's happy-go-lucky voice rang out. "Gregg, we want you to meet our granddaughter, Tangie Carini. She's from Atlantic City."

"Nice to meet you." As he extended his hand, Gregg realized who this must be. Earlier this morning, Dave had said something about counseling a troubled young woman who'd recently joined the church's college and career class. How could Gregg have known she'd turn out to be the grand-daughter of a good friend like Herb Henderson?

His heart broke immediately as he pondered these things. Poor Gramps. How long had he quietly agonized over this granddaughter gone astray? Surely they still had some work ahead of them, based on her bright red hair—were those purple streaks?—and piercings that dazzled.

Not that you could judge a person based on external appearance. He chided himself immediately. He wouldn't want people to make any decisions based on how he looked.

Tangie shook his hand, and then nodded at the papers he'd shoved under his arm. "Great rendition of the 'Hallelujah Chorus.' We performed that my senior year in high school. I'll never forget it."

"Oh? You sing?" When she nodded, he realized at once how he might help the Hendersons get their granddaughter walking the straight and narrow. If she could carry a tune, he'd offer her a position in the choir. Yes, that's exactly what he would do. And if he had to guess, based on her speaking voice, he'd peg her for an alto. Maybe a second soprano.

"We'll see you Sunday, Gregg," Gramps said, patting him on the back. "In fact, it looks like we'll be seeing a lot more of you from now on."

A lot more of me? What's that all about?

Oh yes, Gregg reasoned, it must have something to do with the snows melting. Gramps was anxious to go fishing. Still, the older fellow sure had a strange way of phrasing things.

As Tangie and her grandparents disappeared from view, Gregg made his way to his car. Tonight's date with Ashley would start a whole new chapter of his life. Suddenly, he could hardly wait to turn the page.

three

On Sunday morning, Tangie and her grandparents left for church plenty early. With the roads still covered in snow and ice and Gramps' plan to stop for donuts along the way, they could use the extra time. Besides, she wanted to get to the church in time to acclimate herself to her new surroundings.

Tangie had given herself a quick glance in the mirror just before they left. She'd deliberately chosen her most conservative outfit—a flowing black skirt with a seventies hippie feel to it, and a gray cashmere sweater. Wrapping a black scarf around her neck, she leaned forward to have a look at her makeup. Not too much, not too little. . .just right. She chuckled, realizing how much she sounded like Goldilocks. If only she had the blond hair to make the picture complete. Nah, on second thought, she definitely looked better as a redhead. Or purple, depending on the angle and the lighting.

As they drove to the church, Tangie thought about the events about to transpire. A sense of excitement took hold. The more she thought about it, the more her anticipation grew. This wasn't about shaking people up, as Gran-Gran had said. No, Tangie had come to Harmony to help the kids develop their God-given talents so they could further the kingdom. She wanted to reach people for the Lord, and could clearly see the role the arts played in that. Oh, if only everyone could catch hold of that!

They stopped at the local bakery on the way and Gramps went inside. Tangie and her grandmother chatted while they waited in the Ford.

"I still can't wait to see the looks on everyone's faces when they find out you've been hired as drama director," Gran-Gran said, and then snickered. "Ella Mae Peterson is going to have a fit. She thinks the church spends too much money on their arts programs, as it is."

Tangie sighed. How many times had she heard this argument over the years? "Mrs. Peterson needs to realize the arts are an awesome way to reach people. When you present the gospel message through drama, music, or other artistic venues, people's lives are touched in a way unlike any other. Performing for the Lord isn't about the accolades or even about ability. It's about using the gifts God has given you to captivate the heart and emotions of the audience member. You can't put a price tag on that."

"Exactly." Gran-Gran nodded. "Which is exactly what some of these set-in-their-ways folks need to realize. You're going to shake them up, honey. Give 'em a run for their money."

"Not sure I want to!" she admitted. In fact, this was one time she'd rather just fit in.

"Well, trust me. . .some people could use a little shaking. You'd be surprised how stiff people can be. And I'm not talking arthritis here." Gran-Gran winked.

Stiff? Oh, great. And it's my job to unstiffen them? Just as quickly she chided herself. *No, it's the Lord's job to unstiffen them. . .if He so chooses.*

Gramps returned to the car with a large box of donuts. He reached inside and snagged one, taking a big bite. Gran-Gran scolded him, but he didn't let that stop him. Finishing it, he licked his fingers, then set the car in motion once again.

They arrived at the church in short order. Tangie could hardly believe the mob of cars in the parking lot. "When did this happen, Gran-Gran? It wasn't like this last time I was here."

"Told you! This church is in revival, honey. We're bursting at the seams. Before long, we'll have to build a new sanctuary. In the meantime, we're already holding two Sunday services and one on Saturday evenings, too. Even at that, parking is a mess."

"Wow." Tangie could hardly believe it. Her church in New York City wasn't this full on Sunday mornings, not even on Christmas or Easter.

Once they got inside the foyer, she found herself surrounded on every side by people. "Man, this place has grown."

Gran-Gran flew into action and, over a fifteen-minute period, introduced Tangie to dozens of church members, young and old alike. She met so many people, her head was swimming. Tangie fervently hoped they wouldn't quiz her on the names afterward. She'd fail miserably.

As the word *fail* flitted through her mind, Tangie sighed. *Lord, I don't want to fail at this like I've done so many times.* How many times had she fallen short of the mark in her acting career? How wonderful it would have been to land a lead role just once. She'd dreamed of it all her life, but never quite succeeded. Oh, there had been callbacks. Wonderful, glorious callbacks that got her hopes up. But each time she'd been disappointed, relegated to a smaller role.

On the other hand, Tangie didn't really mind the secondary roles. . .if only they had lasted more than a week or two. So many of the shows she'd been in had closed early, due to poor reviews. Was she destined to remain the underdog forever? Almost good enough. . .but not quite?

And what about her personal life? Would any of her relationships stand the test of time, or would she always bounce from one relationship to the next, never knowing what true love felt like? *I'm asking You to help me succeed this time. Not for my glory, but for Yours. Help me see this thing through from start to finish. I don't want to be a quitter.*

Through the sanctuary doors, she heard the beginning strains of a familiar praise song. As they entered the auditorium, she looked around in amazement. The place was alive with excitement. People clapped their hands along with the music, many singing with abandon. She followed behind Gran-Gran and Gramps to the third row, where they scooted past a couple of people and settled into seats.

Glancing up to the stage, Tangie watched Gregg standing front and center with a guitar in hand. His fingers moved with skill across the strings, and his voice—pure and melodic—immediately ushered her into the presence of God. *See, Lord? That's what I was trying to tell Gran-Gran. It is possible to stand center stage, not for the applause of men, but to bring people closer to You.*

She closed her eyes, thankful for the opportunity to worship. The music continued, each song better than the one before. Tangie watched as the choir geared up for a special number—the contemporary version of the "Hallelujah Chorus." The soloist—a beautiful young woman in her mid-twenties—floored Tangie with her vocal ability.

"That's our children's minister, Ashley Conway," Gran-Gran whispered. "Isn't she something?"

"To say the least," Tangie responded in a hoarse whisper. "I think she rivals anyone I've ever seen or heard on a Broadway stage."

"Yep. We've got some talent here in Harmony, that's for sure." Her grandmother winked before turning to face the stage once again.

Tangie reached for an offering envelope and scribbled the words, "Why doesn't Ashley just help Gregg with the kids' production?" on it. She gave the girl another glance, then penciled in a few more words: "She's got the goods."

Gran-Gran frowned as Tangie handed her the envelope. After reading it, she scribbled down, "Too busy. Ashley works five days a week at the elementary school and Sunday mornings and Wednesday nights at church. No time."

"Ah." Tangie looked up, focusing on the choir. With Gregg at the helm, Ashley and the other choir members performed flawlessly. They were every bit as good as the choir at her home church. Maybe better. And Gregg's heart for God was evident, no doubt about that. Tangie felt shame wash over her as she thought about the way she'd described him to Gran-Gran over the phone.

Lord, forgive me for calling him geeky. This is a great guy. And he's doing a wonderful work here.

In fact, she could hardly wait to work alongside him.

After the choir wrapped up its number, the singers exited the stage. Tangie watched as Gregg trailed off behind them. He reached to pat Ashley on the back, giving a smile and a nod.

"See? He has the gift of encouragement, too," Gran-Gran whispered. "That's a plus."

Finally the moment arrived. Pastor Hampton took the stage. Though she didn't usually struggle with stage fright, Tangie's nerves got the better of her as she listened for his prompting to come to the front of the church for an official introduction to the congregation. As she waited, she narrowed her gaze and focused on Gregg Burke, who now sat in the front row of the next section. He turned back to look at her—or was he looking at Gramps?—with a confused expression on his face. What was up with that?

She found herself staring at him for a moment. Maybe he wasn't as geeky looking as she'd once thought. In fact, that blue shirt really showed off his eyes. . .his best feature.

She'd almost lost her train of thought when Pastor Hampton flashed a smile and said, "I'd like to introduce our new drama director, Tangie Carini." With her knees knocking, she rose from her seat and headed to the stage.

❧

From his spot in the front row, Gregg turned, then stared at the young woman rising from her seat. Wait. *This* was their new drama director? Surely there must be some mistake. The woman Dave had told him about was polished, professional. He would never have described this girl in such a way.

Slow down, Gregg. Don't judge a book by its cover. People did that with your mom, and look what happened.

He forced his thoughts away from that particular subject and watched as Tangie made her way from the pew to the stage. Oh, if only he could stay focused. Her bright red hair—if one could call it red—was far too distracting. Underneath the sanctuary lights, it had a strange purple glow to it. And then there was the row of earrings lining her right ear. Interesting. Different.

She looked his way and offered a shy smile, as if she somehow expected him to know exactly who she was and what she was doing here. He hoped the smile he offered in response was convincing enough.

As she brushed a loose hair from her face, he noticed the tattoo on the inside of her wrist. He strained to make it out, but could not.

"Dave, what have you done?" he whispered. "You've slipped over the edge, man." Tangie Carini was the last person on planet Earth Gregg would've imagined the church hiring. She was the polar opposite of everything. . .well, of everything he was.

On the other hand. . .

As she opened her mouth, thanking the congregation for welcoming her to Harmony Community Church, nothing but pure goodness oozed out. He found himself spellbound by the soothing sound of her voice—very controlled and just the right tone. She'd done this before. . .spoken in front of a crowd.

Then again, if what Dave had said about her was true, she'd performed in front of thousands, and on Broadway, no less. Suddenly Gregg felt like crawling under his pew. Just wait till she got a look at the video of the Christmas play. She'd eat him for lunch.

❧

Tangie shared her heart with the congregation, keenly aware of the fact that Gregg Burke watched her every move. What was he staring at? Surely the pastor had filled him in. . .right?

Oh well. Plenty of time to worry about that later. With a full heart, Tangie began explaining her vision for the drama program.

"I'm a firm believer in stirring up the gifts. And each of these children is gifted in his or her own way. I plan to spend time developing whatever abilities I see in each child so that he or she can walk in the fullness of God's call."

She paused a moment as members of the congregation responded with a couple of "Amens." Looked like they were cool with her ideas thus far.

After that, she went into a passionate speech about the role of the arts in ministry. "God has gifted us for a reason, not for the sake of entertainment—though we all love to entertain and be entertained. However, He has gifted us so that we can share the gospel message in a way that's fresh. Creative. Life-changing."

As she spoke, Tangie noticed the smiles from most in the congregation. Sure, Ella Mae Peterson, Gran-Gran's friend, sat with her arms crossed at her chest. Well, no problem there. She and the Lord would win Mrs. Peterson over.

As she wrapped up her speech, Tangie turned to nod in Gregg's direction. The music pastor flashed a smile, but she noticed it looked a little rehearsed. She knew acting when she saw it. He wasn't happy she was there.

Hmm. Maybe Ella Mae wasn't her only adversary. Well, no problem. Tangie made up her mind to win over Gregg Burke, too. . .no matter what it took.

four

On New Year's Eve, Tangie went with her grandparents to a party at the church. It sure wouldn't be the same as celebrating the New Year in Times Square, but she'd make the best of it. She decided to let her hair down—figuratively speaking—so that the people of Harmony could see the real Tangie. The one with the eclectic wardrobe. She settled on black pants, a 1990s zebra-print top, and a lime green scarf, just for fun. For kicks, she added a hot pink necklace and earring ensemble. Standing back, she took a look at the mirror. "Hmm. Not bad. Nothing like a little color to liven things up."

They'd no sooner arrived at the church than the chaos began. Kids, food, games, activities. . .the whole place was a madhouse. In a happy sort of way.

"Told you we know how to have fun," Gran-Gran said with a twinkle in her eye. "Now, just let me drop off this food in the fellowship hall and I'll introduce you to a few people your own age."

Minutes later, Tangie found herself surrounded by elementary-age kids. They weren't exactly her age, but they'd gravitated to her nonetheless.

A pretty little thing with blond hair tugged at Tangie's sleeve. "I'm Margaret Sanderson and I'm an actress, just like you," the girl said, puffing up her shoulders and tossing her hair. "My mama says I was the best one in the Christmas play. They should've given me the lead part. Then the whole play would've been better."

"Oh? Is that so?" Tangie tried to hold her composure.

"Yes, and I can sing, too." The little girl's confidence increased more with each word. "Want to hear me?"

Before she could respond, the little girl began to belt "The Lullaby of Broadway." To her credit, Margaret could, indeed, sing. And what she lacked in decorum, she made up for in volume. Still, there was something a little over the top about the vivacious youngster.

I know what it is. She reminds me of myself at that age. Only, she's got a lot more nerve.

Tangie released a breath, wanting to say just the right thing. "We'll be holding auditions for an Easter production soon and I certainly look forward to seeing you there."

"Oh, I know. I've been practicing all week," Margaret explained with a knowing look in her eye. "I'm going to be the best one there. And Mama says that if they don't give me the main part, I can't do it at all."

We'll see about that.

Tangie turned as a little boy grabbed her other sleeve. "Hey, do I have to do that stupid Easter play?" he grumbled. "I don't want to."

"Well, I suppose that's up to your mom and dad," she said with a shrug. "It's not my decision."

"I don't have a dad." His gaze shifted downward. "And my mom always makes me try out for these dumb plays. But I stink at acting and singing."

Tangie quirked a brow, wondering where he got such an idea. "Who told you that?"

He stared at her like she'd grown two heads. "Nobody has to tell me. I just stink. Wait till you see the video. Then you'll know."

"Ah. Well, I suppose I'll just have to see for myself, then."

From across the room, Tangie caught a glimpse of Gregg standing next to the young woman who'd sung the solo on Sunday. What did Gran-Gran say her name was again?

Determined to connect with people, Tangie headed their way. As she approached the couple, she could see the look in Gregg's eyes as he talked to the beautiful brunette. Ah. A spark. He must really like her.

Gregg turned Tangie's way and nodded. "Tangie Carini."

"Gregg Burke." She offered a welcoming smile. "We meet officially. . .at last."

"Yes. Sorry about the other day in the hallway. I didn't know who you were, or I would have said something then. I'm glad you're here."

"Thanks." Maybe this wouldn't be as tough as she'd feared. Looked like he was a pretty easygoing guy.

Gregg nodded as he gestured to the brunette at his side. "Tangie, this is Ashley Conway, our children's director."

Ashley. That's it.

Ashley looked her way with curiosity etched on her face. "Tangie?" she said. "I don't think I've ever heard that one before. You'll have to tell me more about your name."

Tangie groaned. Oh, how she hated telling people that she was named after the flavor of the month when she was born. Having parents in the taffy business didn't always work to a girl's advantage.

Thankfully, Pastor Hampton made an announcement, giving her a reprieve.

"I know the kids are anxious to see the video of the Christmas performance," he said. "So why don't we go ahead and gather everyone in the sanctuary to watch it together."

Gregg groaned and Ashley slugged him in the arm. "Oh, c'mon. It's not so bad."

"Whatever." He shook his head, and then looked at Tangie with pursed lips. "Just don't hold this against me, okay? I'm a musician, not a drama director."

"Of course." With anticipation mounting, Tangie tagged along behind Gran-Gran and Gramps to the sanctuary to watch the video. Finally! Something she could really relate to.

"Now, don't expect too much," Gran-Gran whispered as they took their seats. "Remember what I told you on the phone the other day."

"Right." Tangie nodded. Surely her grandmother had exaggerated, though. With Gregg being such an accomplished musician, the production couldn't have been too bad, right?

The lights in the auditorium went down, and she leaned back against her pew, ready for the show to begin. Up on the screen the recorded Christmas production began. Someone had taped the children backstage before the show, going from child to child, asking what he or she thought about the upcoming performance.

"How sweet."

Tangie was particularly struck with the boy who'd approached her in the fellowship hall, the one without a father. Watching him on the screen, she couldn't help but notice how rambunctious he was.

"That's Cody," Gran-Gran said, elbowing her. "One of the rowdy ones that comes with a warning label."

"He's as cute as he can be," Tangie said. She wanted to ruffle his already-messy hair. "I wonder if he can sing."

At that, Gramps snorted. "Wait and see."

"Yikes." Didn't sound promising.

Tangie continued watching the video as the opening music began. The children appeared on the stage and sang a Christmas song together. "Not bad, not bad." Tangie looked at her grandmother and shrugged, then whispered, "What's wrong with that?"

"Keep watching."

At this point, the drama portion of the show began. Tangie almost fell out of her seat when the first child delivered his lines.

"Oh no." He stumbled all over himself. And what was up with that costume? Looked like someone had started it, but not quite finished. At least his was better than the next child's. This precious little girl was definitely wearing something that looked like her mother's bathrobe. It was several inches too long in the arms. In fact, you couldn't see the girl's hands at all.

As she tried to deliver her lines—albeit too dramatically—her sleeves flailed about, a constant distraction.

"Ugh." Tangie shook her head. Only five minutes into the show and she wanted to fix. . .pretty much everything.

At about that time, a little girl dressed as an angel appeared to the shepherds and delivered a line that was actually pretty good. "Oh wait. . .that's the girl I just met," she whispered to her grandmother. "Margaret Sanderson."

"A star in the making," Gran-Gran whispered. "And if you don't believe it, just ask her mother."

Tangie's laugh turned into a honking sound, which she tried to disguise with a cough. Unfortunately, the cough wasn't very convincing, so she resorted to a sneeze. Then hiccups. Before long, several people were looking her way, including Gregg.

Focus, Tangie. Focus.

Turned out, Margaret was the best one in the show. Many of the really good ones came with some degree of attitude. Pride. Oh well. They would work on that. Maybe that's one reason Tangie had come, to help Margaret through this.

Tangie watched once again as Cody took the stage, dressed as a shepherd. Poor kid. He stumbled all over himself, in every conceivable way.

Maybe that's another reason I'm here. He needs a confidence boost.

Funny. One kiddo needed a boost. . .the other needed to be taken down a notch or two.

Oh well, she had it in her. Nothing a little time and TLC couldn't take care of. Determined to make the best of things, Tangie settled in to watch the rest of the show.

❧

Gregg cringed as the video continued. On the night of the performance there had been excitement in the air. It had given him false hope that the show was really not so bad. But tonight, watching the video, he had to admit the truth.

It stunk.

No, it didn't just stink. It was an embarrassment.

He glanced across the aisle at Tangie and her grandparents, wanting to slink from the room. Oh, if only he could read her thoughts right now. Then again, maybe he didn't want to. Maybe it would be best just to pretend she thought it was great.

He watched as Tangie slumped down in her chair. Was she. . .sleeping? Surely not. He tried to focus on the screen, but found it difficult when a couple of people got up and slipped out of the sanctuary, whispering to each other. Great.

Lord, I don't mind admitting this isn't my bag. But I'm feeling pretty humiliated right now. Could we just fast-forward through this part and get right to the next?

Gregg was pretty sure he heard the Lord answer with a very firm, *"No."*

❧

Tangie continued to watch the video, but found the whole thing painful. Gran-Gran had been right. It wasn't just poorly acted; the entire show was lacking in every conceivable way. And talk about dull. How did people stay awake throughout the performance? Looked like half the folks in this place had fallen asleep tonight. Not a good sign.

She glanced across the aisle at Gregg Burke, saddened by the look of pain on his face.

Poor guy. He had to know this wasn't good. Right?

Surely a man with his artistic abilities could see the difference between a good performance and a bad one. And, without a doubt, Gregg Burke was a guy with great artistic skill. By the end of Sunday's service, both his voice and his heart for God had won her over. The way he led the congregation in worship truly captivated her. And though she'd performed on many a stage over the years, Tangie couldn't help but think that leading others into the throne room of God would far surpass any experience she'd ever had in a theater setting.

She snapped back to attention, focusing on the video. For a

moment. As a child on the screen struggled to remember his lines, Tangie's thoughts drifted once again. She pondered her first impression of Gregg—as a stodgy, geeky guy. Tonight, in his jeans and button-up shirt, he was actually quite handsome. Still, he looked a little stiff. Nervous. But why? Did he ever just relax? Enjoy himself?

At that moment, a loud snore to her right distracted her. She looked as Gran-Gran elbowed Gramps in the ribs. Tangie tried not to giggle, but found it difficult. She didn't blame her grandfather for falling asleep. In fact—she yawned as she thought about it—her eyes were growing a little heavy, too.

Before long, she drifted off to sleep, dreaming of badly dressed wise men and Christmas angels who couldn't carry a tune in a bucket.

five

It didn't take Tangie long to settle into a routine at Gran-Gran and Gramps' house. Her creative juices skittered into overtime as she contemplated the task of putting on a show with the children. Oh, what fun it would be. She could practically see it all now! The sets. The costumes. The smiles on the faces of everyone in attendance. With the Lord's help, she would pull off a toe-tapping, hand-clapping musical extravaganza that everyone—kids and church staff, alike—could be proud of.

Tangie received a call from the pastor on Monday morning, asking if they could meet later that afternoon. She stopped off at Sweet Harmony—Gramps' favorite bakery—to pick up some cookies to take to the meeting. Unable to make up her mind, Tangie purchased a dozen chocolate chip, a half dozen oatmeal raisin, and a half dozen peanut butter. Just for good measure, she added a half dozen of iced sugar cookies to her order.

"I can't live without my sweets," she explained to the woman behind the counter. "My family's in the sugar business and I've been in withdrawal since moving away from home."

The clerk—an older woman whose nametag read PENNY—gave her a funny look as she rang up the order. "Sugar business?"

"Yes, we run a candy shop on the boardwalk in Atlantic City, specializing in taffy." Tangie pulled a cookie from the plain white bag and took a big bite. "Mmm. Great peanut butter. They're my favorite."

"You really do have a sweet tooth." Penny laughed as she wiped her hands on her apron. "Well, just so you know, I'm hiring. Sarah, the girl who usually helps me in the afternoons, has gone back to college. So, if you're interested. . ."

"Hmm." Tangie shrugged. "I'll have to see how it works with my schedule. In the meantime, these cookies are great. If you're interested in adding any candies, I'd be happy to talk with you about that. I'd love to bring some of our family favorites to Harmony. I think you'd like them."

"Let me think about it," Penny said. "And you let me know when you've made up your mind about the job. Otherwise, I might put a 'help wanted' sign in the window."

"Give me a couple days to pray about it." Tangie took another bite of the cookie, then headed to her car.

By four o'clock, she and Gregg Burke sat side by side in Dave's spacious office, all three of them nibbling on cookies.

"I'm so excited about what God is doing, I can hardly stand it," Dave said between bites. "We've already got the best music pastor in the world, and now we've just added a Broadway-trained actress to our staff to head up the drama department. Between the two of you, the Easter production is going to be the best thing this community has ever seen."

Tangie felt a little flustered at the pastor's glowing description of her. If he had any idea of the tiny bit parts she'd taken over the past four years, he'd probably rethink his decision. On the other hand. . .

God brought you here, Tangie, she reminded herself. *So don't get in the way of what He's doing.*

"What are you looking for, exactly?" Gregg asked Dave as he reached into the bag for another cookie. "What kind of production, I mean? More of a variety show or an all-out musical?"

"Doesn't really matter. I just want a production that will work hand in hand with the outreach we'll be doing for the community," Dave explained. "I'd like to see something that's different than anything we've done before."

"Different?" Gregg's eyebrows arched as he took another bite. "How different?"

"That's for you two to decide," the pastor said. "We're going to be hosting an Easter egg hunt for the neighborhood kids, as always. But this year we're looking at this as an outreach—the biggest of the year, in fact."

"Easter eggs? Outreach?" Gregg shook his head. "Not sure those two things really go together in one sentence."

"Oh, I think it's a wonderful idea," Tangie said, her excitement mounting. "The Easter egg hunt will be a great draw. And people are always more willing to hear about the Lord during the holidays, so we'll have a captive audience."

Dave nodded. "My thoughts, exactly. We'll advertise the Easter egg hunt in the paper and draw a large crowd. Then, just after the hunt is over, we'll open up the auditorium for everyone to come inside for the production. It will be free, of course."

"I think that's a wonderful idea," Tangie said. "That way all of the kids can watch the show, even the ones who wouldn't be able to afford it otherwise."

"You've got it!" Dave looked at her and beamed.

Clearly, they were on the same page.

She looked at Gregg, hoping for a similar response. He sat with a confused expression on his face. What was up with that?

"I don't really have anything specific in mind, as far as what kind of production it should be," the pastor continued, "just something that appeals to kids and shares the real meaning of Easter in a tangible way. But different, as I said. Something kid-friendly and contemporary."

Gregg looked a little dubious. "How will we get the kids and their families to stay for the musical? I can see them coming for the Easter egg hunt, maybe, but how do we get them inside the building once it's over?"

"I've been thinking about that." Dave rolled a pen around in his fingers. "Haven't exactly come up with anything yet, though."

"Oh, I know," Tangie said. "Maybe we could do some sort of a drawing for a grand prize. A giant Easter egg, maybe? The winner to be announced after the production. That might entice them to stay."

"Giant Easter egg?" Gregg asked.

"Made of chocolate, of course." Tangie turned to him, more excited than ever. "At my family's candy shop, we have these amazing eggs. . .oh, you have to see one to believe it! They're as big as a football. No, bigger. And they're solid chocolate, hand decorated by my sister. I know Taffie will help. She loves things like this."

"Taffy will help?" Gregg looked at Tangie curiously. "What does that mean?"

"Oh, sorry." She giggled and her cheeks warmed. "Taffie is my older sister. There are three of us—Taffie, Candy, and me."

"Tangie." Dave said with a smile. "Your grandmother told me they sometimes call you Tangerine, just to be funny."

"Terrific." Tangie groaned. "As you might imagine, Tangie wouldn't have been my first choice for a name. How would you feel if you were named after the flavor of the month when you were born?"

Gregg chuckled, offering Tangie her first glimmer of hope from the beginning of the meeting till now. His eyes sparkled and a hint of color rose to his cheeks. "So, we're giving away an egg, then?" he asked.

"If that's okay with both of you." Tangie looked back and forth between them "They sell for a fortune, but I'm sure Taffie would send one for free, especially if I tell her what it's for. My sister and her husband love the Lord and would be thrilled to see one of their candy eggs used for ministry."

"Eggs for ministry." Gregg groaned and shook his head. "What's next?"

"Oh, that's easy." Tangie nodded. "Sheep, bunnies, and chicks, of course. And anything else that might appeal to little kids. Oh"—her heart swelled with joy as the words tumbled out—"this is going to be the best Easter ever!"

❧

Gregg watched with some degree of curiosity as Tangie and Dave talked back and forth about the production. Talk about feeling like a third wheel. Why was he here, anyway? He did his best not to struggle with any offense. He'd been through enough of that as a kid. No, in fact, he looked forward to Tangie's help with the production, though he still had a hard time admitting it to anyone other than himself.

Still, that bunnies and chicks line had to be a joke. Right?

Listening to her talk, her voice as animated as her facial expression, he had the strangest feeling. . .she was dead serious.

He glanced at his watch and gasped. "Oh, sorry to cut this short, but I've got a date with my mom. I'm taking her to the movies this afternoon."

"A date with your mom?" Tangie flashed a smile. He couldn't tell if she was making fun of him or found the idea thoughtful. Not that it really mattered. No, where his mom was concerned, only one thing mattered. . .convincing her that the Lord loved her. And there was only one way to accomplish that really. . .by spending quality time with her and loving her, himself. Not an easy task sometimes, what with her brusque exterior. But Gregg was really working on not judging people by outward appearance, especially his own mom.

"When can we meet to talk about the production?" Tangie asked. "One day this week?"

"Mornings are better for me," he said as he rose from his chair. "What about Thursday?"

"Thursday it is. Where?"

"Hmm." He reached for his coat. "The diner on Main? They've got a great breakfast menu. Very inspirational. I'm going to need it if we're talking about putting on a show, trust me."

Tangie grinned. "Okay. I'll see you there. Will seven thirty work?"

"Yep." He nodded. "Sorry I have to bolt, but my mom is expecting me." After a quick goodbye, he headed toward the car, his thoughts whirling in a thousand different directions.

six

Tangie pulled herself out of bed early on Thursday morning and dressed in one of her favorite outfits—a pair of faded bell-bottoms and a great vintage sweater she'd picked up at a resale shop—a throwback from the 1960s in varying shades of hot pink, orange, and brown. Why anyone would've parted with it was beyond her. Sure, the colors were a little faded, but that just gave it a more authentic look. And coupled with the shiny white vinyl go-go style boots, which she'd purchased for a song, the whole ensemble just came together. Once you added in the hat. She especially loved the ivory pillbox-style hat with its mesh trim. Marti said it reminded her of something she'd once seen on *I Love Lucy*. What higher compliment was there, really?

Tangie made her way into the living room, laptop in hand.

Gramps took one look at her and let out a whistle. "I haven't seen a getup like that since Woodstock. Not that I went to Woodstock, mind you."

"I believe I wore a little hat just like that on our wedding day," her grandmother added. "Wherever did you find that?"

"Oh, I get the best bargains at resale shops," Tangie said with a nod. "Who wants to shop at the mall? The clothes are so. . ."

"Normal?" her grandfather threw in.

Tangie laughed. "Maybe to you, but I think I'll stick with what makes me feel good."

"And all of that color makes you feel good?"

"Yep." In fact, on days like today—dressed in the colorful ensemble—she felt like she had the world on a string.

After saying goodbye to her grandparents, she eased her car out of the slick driveway. As she drove through town,

Tangie passed Sweet Harmony and smiled as she remembered meeting Penny. What a great lady.

"Lord, what do You think about that job offer? Should I take it?" Hmm. She'd have to pray about that a bit longer. In the meantime, she had one very handsome music pastor to meet with.

Handsome? Tangie, watch yourself.

She sighed, thinking of how many leading men she'd fallen in love with over the past four years. Taffie and Candy had always accused her of being fickle, but. . .was she? After less than a second's pause, she had to admit the truth. She *had* been pretty flighty where talented guys were concerned. And the more talented, the harder she seemed to fall. All the more reason *not* to fall for Gregg Burke.

Not that he was her type, anyway. No, he seemed a little too "in the box" for her liking.

She arrived at the diner a few minutes early, but noticed Gregg's SUV in the parking lot. "He's very prompt," she said to herself. Pulling down the visor, she checked her appearance in the tiny mirror. Hmm. The eyeliner might be a bit much. She'd gone for a forties look. But she'd better touch up the lipstick to match in intensity. Tangie pulled it from her purse and gave her lips a quick swipe, then rubbed them together as she gazed back in the mirror. "Better."

Then, slip-sliding her way along, Tangie made the walk across the icy parking lot, cradling her laptop and praying all the way. She arrived inside the diner, stunned to find it so full. Gregg waved at her from the third booth on the right and she headed his way. As she drew near, his eyes widened.

"What?" she asked, as she put her laptop down, then shrugged off her jacket.

"N—nothing." He paused, his gaze shifting to her hat. "I, um, just don't think I've ever seen a hat like that in person. In the movies, maybe. . ."

"I'll take that as a compliment." She laughed, then took her seat. Glancing around, she said, "You were right. This place is hopping."

"Oh, this is nothing. Most of the breakfast crowd has already passed through. You should see it around six thirty or seven." He continued to stare at her hat and she grew uncomfortable. Should she take it off? Maybe it was distracting him.

"The food must be good," Tangie managed. She reached to unpin her hat just as a young waitress appeared at the table and smiled at her.

"Oh, please don't take off that hat! It's amazing!"

Tangie grinned and left it in place.

The girl's face lit up. "You're Tangie Carini."

Tangie nodded.

"I knew it had to be you. That's the coolest outfit I've ever seen, by the way. Seriously. . .where did you get it? Is that what they're wearing on the runway this season?"

"Thanks. And, no. This is just vintage stuff. I love to shop in out-of-the-way places."

"I have a feeling I'm really going to like you," the waitress said. "I've been wanting to meet you ever since I heard you speak in church on Sunday morning."

"Oh?" Tangie took the menu the girl offered and glanced up at her with a smile. "Why is that?"

"Brittany is one of the leaders of the youth group," Gregg explained. "She was a big help to me with the Christmas production."

"I've always been interested in theater," Brittany said. "Our high school did *The Sound of Music* my sophomore year."

"She played Maria," Gregg said. "And she was pretty amazing."

Brittany's cheeks turned red. "My favorite role was Milly in *Seven Brides for Seven Brothers*. We did that show my senior year, and I loved every minute of it."

"Oh, that's one of my favorites," Tangie said. "I played the role of Milly at our local community theater back in Atlantic City."

"Oh, I can't believe you just said that!" Brittany clasped her hands together and grinned. "This is a sign from above. A community theater is exactly what I wanted to talk to you about." Brittany's eyes lit up and her tone of voice changed. She grew more animated by the second. "Several of us have been wanting to start a community theater group here in Harmony. There's an old movie theater that would be perfect. It's not in use any more, but would be great. Just needs a stage."

"Do you have funding?"

Brittany shrugged. "Never really thought about that part. I guess we could hold a fund-raiser or something like that. But I'd love to talk to you more about it. Maybe. . ." The teenager flashed a crooked grin. "Maybe you could even direct some of our shows."

"Ah ha." *I see.* So, that's what this was about. First she was directing at the church, now a community theater? *Lord, what are You up to, here? Trying to keep me in Harmony forever?*

Just then, the manager passed by and Brittany snapped to attention. "Are you ready to order?" she asked, grabbing her notepad and pen.

"I'll have two eggs over easy, bacon, toast, and hot tea," Tangie said.

"I'll have the same." Gregg closed his menu. "But make mine coffee. I'm not into the tea thing."

Brittany took their menus and headed to the kitchen.

"She's a great kid," Gregg said. "Very passionate about the theater. Hoping to go to New York one day."

"She's really talented, then?"

"She's pretty good, but I don't think she realizes what she'd be up against in the Big Apple."

"I could fill her in, but it might be discouraging," Tangie said with a shrug.

"So, you didn't just jump into lead roles right away?" he asked, peering into her eyes.

Tangie couldn't help but laugh. "I didn't jump into lead

roles, period. Trust me, I was fortunate to land paying gigs at all, large or small. And they didn't last very long, sometimes. A couple of the shows I was in folded after just a few performances. Life in the theater can be very discouraging."

He shrugged, and his gaze shifted down to the table. "I guess it's the same in the music industry. I tried recording a CD a few years ago, but couldn't get any radio stations to play my tunes. Pretty sobering, actually."

"Man, they don't know what they're missing." Tangie shook her head, trying to imagine why anyone would turn Gregg's music away. "You've got one of the most anointed voices I've ever heard."

"Really? Thanks." He seemed stupefied by her words, but she couldn't figure out why. Surely others had told him how powerful those Sunday morning services were, right?

Brittany returned with a coffee pot in hand. She filled Gregg's mug. Then she started to pour some in Tangie's cup, but stopped just as a dribble of the hot stuff tumbled into the cup. "Oops, sorry. You said you wanted tea."

"Yes, please." When Brittany left, Tangie smiled at Gregg. "It's funny. I love the smell of coffee, but I don't really like the way it tastes. My roommate back in New York used to drink three or four cups a day."

"It's great early in the morning." He took a sip, then leaned back in his seat, a contented look on his face. "I've been addicted since I was in my late teens. My mom. . ." He hesitated. "Well, my mom sometimes let me do a few of the grown-up things a little earlier than most."

"Speaking of your mom, how did your date go?"

He laughed. "Good. She's a hoot. You'll have to meet her someday."

"Does she go to the church? Maybe I've met her already."

"The church?" Gregg's brow wrinkled. "No. I wish. But I'm working on that."

"So, she let you have coffee as a kid?" Tangie asked, going

back to the original conversation.

"Yes." He grinned. "First thing in the morning, we'd each have two cups. Then she'd leave for work and I'd get on the bus to go to school. Wide awake, I might add."

"Well, maybe that was the problem. I was never up early in the morning when I lived in New York. I rarely got to bed before three or four and usually slept till ten or eleven in the morning. By the time I got up and running, it was practically lunchtime."

"Are you a night owl?" Gregg asked.

"Always have been." She smiled, remembering the trouble she'd gotten in as a kid. "So, life in the theater just works for me. . .at least on some levels. Shows never end till really late, and there's always something going on after."

"Like what?"

"Oh, dinner at midnight with other cast members." Tangie allowed her thoughts to ramble for a moment. She missed her roomie, Marti, and their midnight meetings at Hanson's twenty-four-hour deli after each show.

"I've always been a morning person," Gregg said. "Sounds crazy, but evenings are tough on me. When nine o'clock rolls around, I'm ready to hit the hay."

"That's so funny." Tangie tried not to laugh, but the image of someone dozing off at nine was humorous, after the life she'd led in the big city. She paused and then opened her laptop. "I guess we should get busy, huh?"

Gregg's expression changed right away. Gone were the laugh lines around his eyes. In their place, a wrinkled brow and down-turned lips.

Tangie studied his expression, sensing his shift in attitude. "You're not looking forward to this?"

He shrugged and offered a loud sigh in response. "In case you didn't notice from that video you watched, I'm not exactly a pro at putting on shows with kids. If we could sing our way through the whole performance, fine, but anything with lines and costumes sends me right over the edge."

"Well, that's why I'm here." She grinned, feeling the excitement well up inside her. "I want you to know I'm so hyped up about all of this, I could just. . .throw a party or something."

"Really?" He looked at her as if he didn't quite believe it.

"Yes, I don't know how to explain it, but there's something about putting on a show that makes my heart sing. I love every minute of it—the auditions, reading the script for the first time, building the set, memorizing lines. . ." She paused, deep in thought, then said, "Of course, I'm usually the one on the stage, not the one directing, but I have worked with kids before and I just know this will be a ton of fun."

"Humph." He crossed his arms at his chest and leaned back against his seat. "If you say so. I'd rather eat a plateful of artichokes—my least favorite food on planet Earth, by the way—than put on another show. But we'll get through this." He reached for his cup of coffee and took a swig, then shrugged.

"Oh, we'll more than get through it," she promised him. Reaching to rest her hand on his, she gave him a knowing look. "By the end of this, you're going to be a theater buff, I promise."

Gregg laughed. "If you can pull *that* off, I'll eat a whole plate of artichokes. In front of every kid in the play."

"I'm not going to let you forget you said that." Tangie nodded, already planning for the event in her head. "I'm going to hold you to it." She glanced at her laptop screen, and then looked back up at him. "In the meantime, we should probably talk about the production. I had the most wonderful idea for the Easter play. I hope you like it."

"Wait." He shook his head. "You mean, you actually wrote something? Already?"

"Well, of course. You didn't expect me to get one of those canned musicals from the Bible bookstore, did you?"

He shrugged. "I didn't know there was any other way."

Tangie laughed. "Oh, you really don't know me. I don't do anything by the book. And while there are some great productions out there, I really felt like Pastor Dave wanted us to cater specifically to the community, using the Easter egg hunt as our theme. Didn't you?"

Another shrug from Gregg convinced her he hadn't given the idea much thought.

"Well, I don't know about all that," he said. "And I definitely think a traditional Easter pageant is the safest bet. People expect to see certain things when they come for an Easter production, don't you think?" He began to list some of the elements he hoped to see in the show and Tangie leaned back, realizing her dilemma at once.

She eventually closed her laptop and focused on the animation in Gregg's voice as he spoke. He hadn't been completely honest with her earlier, had he? All of that stuff about how he didn't like doing performances wasn't true at all. Right now, listening to him talk about his version of an Easter pageant—which, to her way of thinking, sounded incredibly dull—she could see the sparkle in his eye. The tone of his voice changed.

In that moment, she realized the truth. It wasn't that he didn't like putting on shows. He just hadn't done one he could be proud of. That's all. But if they moved forward with the pageant he had in mind, things were liable to fall apart again. She didn't see—or hear—anything in his plan that sounded like what Pastor Dave asked for.

Tangie swallowed hard, working up the courage to speak. *Lord, show me what to say. I don't want to burst his bubble, but we're supposed to be doing something different. Something original.*

When he finally paused, Tangie exhaled and then looked into his eyes, noticing for the first time just how beautiful they were.

He gazed back, a boyish smile on his face. His cheeks

flushed red and he whispered, "Sorry. Didn't mean to get carried away."

"Oh, don't be sorry." She hated to burst his bubble, but decided to add her thoughts. "I, um, was thinking of something completely different than what you described, though."

"Oh? Like what?"

"Well, hear me out. What I've written is really unique, something people have never seen before."

He gave her a dubious look.

"Just don't laugh, okay?" She proceeded to tell him about her plan to use talking animals—sheep, bunnies, baby chicks, and so forth—to convey the message of Easter.

"I've been thinking about this whole egg theme," she explained. "And I think we need to start the show with a giant Easter egg—maybe four or five feet high—in the center of the stage. We'll get some really cute kid-themed music that fits the scene, and the egg can crack open and a baby chick will come out. Of course, it'll be one of the kids, dressed as a chick. He—or she—can be the narrator, telling the rest of the story. There's going to be a shepherd, of course. He'll represent God. We'll need an adult for that. And then the little sheep—and we'll need lots of them—will be us, His kids. Make sense?"

Gregg stared at her like she'd lost her mind. Still, Tangie forged ahead, emphasizing the takeaway at the end of the play.

"See? It's an allegory," she explained. "A story inside a story. The baby chick hatching from its egg represents us, when we're born again. We enter a whole new life. Our story begins, in essence. The same is true with rabbits. Did you realize that bunnies are symbols for fertility and rebirth?"

"Well, no, but I guess I can see the parallel," he said. "Rabbits rapidly reproduce."

"Say *that* three times in a row." Tangie laughed.

He tried it and by the end, they were both chuckling.

Once she caught her breath, Tangie summed up her

thoughts about the play. "So, the chicks and the bunnies are symbols of the rebirth experience. And the bunnies—because they rapidly reproduce—will be our little evangelists. Get it? They'll hop from place to place, sharing the love of Jesus."

"Um, okay."

"And the little sheep represent us, too. One of them wanders away from the fold and Jesus—the shepherd—goes after him. Or her. I haven't decided if it should be a boy or girl. But there's that hidden message of God's love for us. . .that He would leave the ninety-nine to go after the one. I think the audience will get it if they're paying attention."

"Maybe." He shook his head. "But I don't know about all that. I still think it's better to do something tried and true."

"Like your Christmas play?" Tangie could've slapped herself the minute the words came out. "I–I'm sorry."

He shook his head. "I've already admitted that I'm no director."

"I'm sure that's not true," she said. "You just haven't found the right show yet. But I think this Easter production has the capability of turning things around for both the kids who are in it and the ones who come to see it." She offered what she hoped would be taken as a winning smile. "And you'll see. By the end of this, you're going to fall in love with theater. It won't just be a means to an end anymore. It's going to get into your blood. You'll be hooked."

"Somehow I really doubt it." Gregg took a swig of his coffee and gave her a pensive look. "But, for lack of a better plan, I'll go along with this little chicks and bunnies play you're talking about. Just don't credit me with writing any of it, okay?"

He dove into a lengthy discussion about how he'd already been embarrassed enough with the last play and how he had no intention of being the subject of ridicule again. Tangie listened in stunned silence, realizing just how strongly he felt about her ideas, in spite of her persuasive argument, seconds earlier. But, why? Was it just her ideas he didn't like. . .or her?

Tangie's heart plummeted to her toes. Not only did he not like her ideas, he acted like he thought she was crazy. Well, she'd show him a thing or two about crazy over the next few weeks. And then, if she ended up failing at this gig in Harmony...she might just give some thought to heading back home...to the Big Apple.

ಎ

Gregg could've slapped himself for making fun of Tangie in such a pointed way. From the look in her eyes, he knew he'd injured her pride. He knew just what that felt like. Still, he wasn't sure how to redeem the situation now. *Lord, I'm going to need Your help with this one. It's beyond me.*

Yes, everything about this was beyond him—the production, the outreach...and the beautiful woman in the nutty outfit seated across from him with the look of pain in her eyes.

seven

"Gran-Gran, you know I love you, right?" Tangie paced her grandparents' living room as she spoke with great passion.

"Of course!" Her grandmother looked up from the TV and nodded. "But you're blocking the TV, honey. We're trying to watch *Jeopardy*."

Tangie sighed and took a giant step to the left. Nothing ever got between Gran-Gran and her TV when the game shows were on. Still, this was important. Tangie attempted to interject her thoughts. "Gran-Gran, you know I would never do anything to hurt you."

"Never."

"What is *the Sears Tower*!" Gramps hollered at the TV.

Tangie looked his way and he shrugged. "Sorry, honey. The question was, 'What is the tallest building in America?' and I happened to know the answer."

He and Gran-Gran turned back to the TV, and Tangie knew she'd lost them. She took a seat on the sofa and sighed. Gran-Gran looked her way.

"You're really upset, aren't you?"

Tangie nodded. "Sort of." She worked up the courage to say the rest. "Now, don't be mad, but I'm giving some thought to only staying in Harmony till after the production, then going back to New York."

"What?" Her grandmother turned and looked at her with a stunned expression on her face, then reached for the remote and flipped off the TV. "But why?"

How could she begin to explain it in a way that a non-theater person could understand? "I. . .I need artistic freedom." There. That should do it.

"Artistic freedom?" Gramps rose from his well-worn recliner and snagged a cookie from the cookie jar. "What did someone do, kidnap your creativity or something?"

"Very nicely put," she said. "That's exactly what someone did. He stole it and put it behind bars. And as long as I stay in Harmony, I'm never getting it back. I'm destined to be dull and boring."

Her grandmother's brows elevated slightly. "You? Dull and boring? Impossible." Gran-Gran stood up and approached Tangie.

"I can see how it would happen here," Tangie said. "I feel like my voice has been squelched."

"Impossible. You've got too much chutzpah for that. Besides, folks can only take what you give, nothing more."

"Maybe I just don't know enough about how to compromise with someone like Gregg Burke. But one thing is for sure, this gig in Harmony doesn't feel like a long-term plan for me."

Gran-Gran's eyes misted over right away. "Are you serious?"

"Yes." Tangie sighed when she saw the hurt look on her grandmother's face. "I'll stay till the Easter production is over at the beginning of April. But then I'm pretty sure I'd like to go back to New York."

"Really? But I thought you were done with New York," Gramps said, a confused look on his face.

"Well, see, I got an e-mail from my friend Marti last night. She just found out about auditions for a new show. They're going to be held a few days after the production and the director, Vincent, is an old friend of mine. He directed a couple of plays I was in year before last. I'll stand a better shot with this one, since I know someone."

"Honey, I know you enjoy being in those shows. You're a great little actress."

Tangie cringed at the words *little actress*. How many times had her father said the same thing? And her directors? She didn't want to be a *little* actress. She wanted to have a career. A real career.

Gran-Gran continued, clearly oblivious to Tangie's inner turmoil. "But, as good as you are, that's not your ministry. You're a teacher. You said it yourself when you stood up in front of the church to talk to the congregation. You're a gift stirrer. Your real ability is in motivating and teaching those kids. And if you go away. . ." Gran-Gran's eyes filled with tears. "Well, if you go away, nothing will be the same around here. There's no one to take your place."

Tangie shrugged. "Gregg will do fine. And Ashley. . .she's great with the kids."

"Yes, but she's too busy. That's what I was saying before. She has a full-time job at the school, teaching second grade."

"Right." Tangie sighed.

"That's why she couldn't help with the Christmas production. She was doing a show of her own. I know her pretty well, honey. She would probably agree to help, just to appease Gregg, but she's just too overwhelmed to take on anything else right now."

"I'm sorry, Gran-Gran. I just don't think I'm up for the job long term. It's going to be hard enough to make it through one show." Tangie tried not to let the defeat show on her face but couldn't seem to help herself.

Gran-Gran plopped down in a chair, a somber look on her face. "Well, I'm sorry to hear that. Very sorry."

As she left the room, Tangie reached for an oatmeal raisin cookie—her third. She took a big bite, pondering everything her grandmother had said. Looked like Tangie was right all along. She wasn't meant for small-town life.

What did it matter, really? Apparently she was destined to fail at everything she put her hand to—whether it was in the big city or in a tiny place like Harmony, New Jersey.

❧

Gregg picked up the phone and called Gramps for a much-needed chat. The elderly man answered on the third ring, his opening words packing quite a punch. "What took you so long, son?"

"H—hello?"

"I know it's you, Gregg. Saw your number on the caller ID. I've been sitting by the phone for the past hour, ever since Tangie talked to us about that meeting you two had at the diner this morning. She was plenty worked up."

"Oh, I'm sorry," Gregg started. "I—"

"Ruined a perfectly good round of *Jeopardy*," Gramps interrupted. "I figured you would've called me before this."

Gregg groaned. "I guess I should have. Things didn't go very well."

"So I hear. There's actually talk of her leaving. Going back to New York City. I'd hate to see that happen. Why, the very idea of it is breaking my heart."

"No way." She was giving up. . .that quickly? Why? "Can you put her on the phone, please?" Gregg asked.

He heard Gramps' voice ring out, "Tangie, you've got a call."

Seconds later, she answered. "Taffie, what happened? Everything okay with the baby?"

"Taffy?" Gregg repeated. "What does taffy have to do with anything?"

"O—oh, I'm sorry. I thought for sure Gramps said my sister was on the phone. Who is this?"

"Gregg Burke."

"Oh." The tone of her voice changed right away. In fact, her initial excitement fizzled out like air from a flat tire.

"I'm calling to apologize," he said, his words coming a mile a minute. "I've really messed this one up. Please don't go anywhere. I need you too much for that."

"You do?"

"Yes." He sighed. Might as well just speak his mind. "To be honest, I think I'm just insecure. I don't know the first thing about drama, but it's still hard to admit that I'm a failure at anything. Does that make sense?"

"More than you know."

"I think my pride was a little hurt, is all. I'll be the first to admit it." He paused a moment. "Your ideas about the Easter play are. . .different. Very different from anything I would've come up with. But maybe that's why they hired you. They want different. And this is for kids. Kids need kid stuff, and I'll be honest, I don't know the first thing about kid stuff. I think I proved that with the Christmas play."

"Well, I'm different, all right," Tangie responded. "But I don't want you to think I'm so off the wall that I'm going to end up embarrassing you or the kids in any way. That's not my intention. I can see this production being really cute, but if you'd rather do something more traditional. . ." Her words faded away.

"No, it's fine. I just think we need to meet to get this settled, one way or the other. Can you send me a copy of what you've written by e-mail attachment? I'll take a look at it and see what I can do with it from a music standpoint. Then we can talk again before next week's auditions. How does that sound?"

She hesitated, but finally came back with, "Good. Thanks for giving me a second chance."

"No." He sighed. "I shouldn't have been so quick to shut you down the first time. I'm just used to being the creative one, and you. . ."

She laughed. "I know, I know. When God handed out creativity, He gave me a double portion. I've never understood why."

"Oh, I think I do," Gregg said. "He knew He could trust you with it."

She paused for a moment and then a much quieter Tangie came back with, "Thank you. That's the nicest thing anyone's said to me in a long time. I needed to hear that."

By the time they ended the call, Gregg felt a hundred pounds lighter. Until he thought about the giant Easter egg she'd proposed for the opening scene. Then his stomach began to tighten once again. *Lord, this is going to be. . .different. Give me patience. Please.*

❧

Tangie sighed as she hung up the phone. Gregg's plea for help had surprised her, especially after his reaction this morning. Who put him up to this?

"Gramps?" She called out for her grandfather, but he didn't answer. Tangie looked around the living room, but couldn't find him anywhere, so she bundled up in her coat and headed out to his workshop behind the house. There she found him, carving a piece of wood.

"Oh, wow." She looked around the tiny room, amazed by all of the things she found there. "You're very crafty, Gramps."

"That's what they tell me." He held out a wood-carved replica of a bear and smiled. "What do you think of this guy?"

"I think he's great. I also think. . ." The idea hit her all at once. "I also think I'm going to use your services for the kids' production."

"So, you're sticking around? Gregg did the right thing?"

"I'm sticking around." She shrugged. "I would've stayed till after the play anyway, remember?"

"Now you'll stay longer?"

She sighed and rested against his workbench, thankful for the tiny space heater at her feet. "I can't make any promises. Who knows where things will be in a few months? There's this really great show. . ."

"I know, I know." He sighed, then reached to give her a peck on the cheek. "In New York. A chance of a lifetime. Something you've been waiting for. . .forever." He stressed the word *forever*, making it seem like a mighty long time.

"I know you want me to stay here," Tangie said. "And I promise to pray about it."

"That's all I ask, honey." He nodded and smiled. "But let me say one more thing." Gramps peered into her eyes, his gaze penetrating to her very soul. "Your mother isn't the only one with a case of wanderlust."

"What?"

"I mean, you have a hard time staying put in one place for long. And with one job for long." He paused. "Now, I don't mean anything negative by that; it's just an observation. Maybe your trip to Harmony is a lesson in staying put awhile."

"Hmm." She shrugged. "I don't know, Gramps. I just know that I always get this jittery feeling. And bolting is. . ."

"Easier?"

"Sometimes." She sighed. "I'm sure you're right. It's a learned behavior. I wasn't always this way. But when one show after another shut down, I just got in the habit of shifting gears. Now I've turned so many corners, I can hardly remember where I've been and where I'm going. And bolting just comes naturally. I'm not proud of it. I'm just saying it's become second nature, that's all."

"Well, pray before you bolt. That's all I ask this time." He wrapped her in his arms and placed a whiskery kiss in her hair. " 'Cause when you leave this time, it's gonna break some poor fella's heart." He dabbed his eyes, then whispered, "And I'm not just talking about Gregg Burke's."

eight

On Friday morning, Tangie stopped off at Sweet Harmony, the bakery where she'd purchased the cookies. Penny greeted her with a welcoming smile.

"Great coat. Love the shoulder pads. Very 1980s."

"Thanks." Tangie chuckled. "That's the idea. I love wearing clothes from every era."

"Kind of reminds me of something Joan Collins would've worn in *Dynasty*." Penny paused, then gave Tangie a pensive look. "Been thinking about that proposition I made?"

"I have." Tangie smiled. "I think I'd like to work here, but I might only be staying in town till the first week in April. Would that be a problem?"

"Hmm." Penny shrugged and wiped her hands on her apron. "Well, I can really use the help, even if it's temporary. I'll take what I can get."

"We'll need to come to some agreement about my schedule. I'm working part-time at a local church."

"Church?" Penny rolled her eyes. "I used to go to a church... back in the day."

"Whatever happened with that?" Tangie asked.

Penny shrugged. "Gave it up for Lent." She slapped herself on the knee and let out a raucous laugh. "Oh, that's a good one. Gave up church for Lent." After a few more chuckles, she finally calmed down. "Let's just say God and I aren't exactly on speaking terms and leave it at that."

"Ah."

"And I guess I could also add that the church hasn't exactly laid out the welcome mat for me. But, mind you, I haven't been to one since I was in my thirties, so I'm not talking about any church in particular here. I just know that churches, in general, don't take too kindly to unmarried women with kids."

"Whoa. Really?" Tangie thought about that for a moment. Most of the churches she'd attended—both at home in Atlantic City and in New York—had always reached out to single moms. But it looked like Penny had a different story. Then again, Penny was—what?—in her late fifties, maybe? So, anything that happened to her had to have happened twenty or thirty years ago, right?

"Back to the bakery. . ." Penny gave her a scrutinizing glance. "How are your cake decorating skills?"

Tangie shrugged. "We didn't do much pastry work at the candy shop, but I've decorated cookies and other sweets, and I've got a steady hand."

"You're hired."

"Just like that?" Tangie laughed. "You don't need references or anything?"

"Your grandfather is Herbert Henderson?" Penny stared at her thoughtfully.

"Yes. How did you know that?"

"He's my best customer, and he's been telling me all about this granddaughter of his from the candy shop in Atlantic City. He described you to a tee, right down to the tattoo on your wrist. What is that, anyway? A star?"

"Yeah." Tangie shrugged. "A theater friend of mine talked me into it years ago. She said I was going to be a big star someday, and that looking at my wrist would be a good reminder not to give up."

"Have you?"

"W–what?"

"Given up?" Penny gave her a pensive look.

"Oh, no. Not really. I, um, well, I'm just on hiatus from acting right now."

"Okay." Penny pursed her lips, then spoke in a motherly

voice. "Just don't let me hear that you've given up on your dreams. You need to go after them. . .wholeheartedly. I let mine die for a while." She looked around the bakery, then grinned. "But eventually got around to it. Just wasted a lot of time in between."

"I understand. And part of the reason I'm in Harmony is to figure all of that out."

"Well, if Herbert Henderson is really your grandfather, I'd say you'll have a lot of wise counsel. He's a crackerjack, that one."

"You know him well?" Tangie asked, taking a seat at one of the barstools in front of the counter.

"He buys kolaches and donuts for his Sunday school class every Sunday morning. He's got quite a sweet tooth. My boys were always partial to sweets, too."

"Tell me about your boys." Tangie leaned against the countertop, ready to learn more about her new friend.

"What's to tell? They're boys. And besides, if you go to your grandpa's church, you probably know at least one of them."

"Wait. Who?"

"My oldest, Gregg. He plays the guitar and sings."

Tangie stared at Penny, stunned. "Gregg Burke. . .is your son?"

"Well, sure. I thought you knew that. Figured your grandfather told you."

"Grandpa didn't say anything." Tangie would have to remember to throttle him later. How interesting, that she would end up working with Gregg at the church and with his mother at the bakery.

She startled back to attention. Turning to her new boss, she asked, "When would you like me to start?"

Penny reached behind the counter and came up with an apron with the words SWEET HARMONY emblazoned on the front. "How about right now? I've got to make a run to the doctor in Trenton."

"Trenton?"

"Yep. Planned to close the place down for the rest of the day, but I'd rather leave it open, if you're up to it. Can you handle the register until I get back?"

"Mmm, sure." Tangie slipped the apron over her head. "I operated the cash register at our candy store for years as a teen. Anything else?"

"Yes, let me run over a few things with you." Penny quickly went over the price list, focusing on the special of the day—two cream-filled donuts and hot cocoa for three dollars. Then she gave Tangie a quick tour of the building. When they finished, the older woman turned to her with a smile. "Do you think you'll be okay?"

"Should be."

"Great. Oh, one more thing. When the timer goes off, pull those cookies out of the oven and set them on the rack to cool." Penny pointed to the tall chrome double oven and then reached for her purse. "Wish I didn't have to go at all, but I won't be long." She took a few steps toward the door, but then turned back. "Oh, and if you see an older fellow—about my age—with white hair and a thick moustache, don't sell him a thing."

"W–what? Why?" Tangie asked.

"That's Bob Jennings. He's a diabetic. Comes in nearly every afternoon around this time, begging for sweets. His wife would kill me if I actually sold him anything."

"Why don't you offer sugar-free options?" Tangie asked. "We sell a whole line of sugar-free candies at our store."

Penny put her hands on her hips. "See! That's why I need you. Now that you're here. . ." Her voice faded as the door slammed closed behind her. Tangie watched through the plate-glass window as Penny scurried down the sidewalk toward the parking lot, talking to herself.

"Lord, how am I going to give her all of the help she needs in only three months?" Three years might be more workable. Still, all of that stuff about not giving up on your dreams. . .

was the Lord speaking through Penny, perhaps? Stranger things had happened. Maybe God's plan for Tangie included at least one more shot at Broadway.

"April." She whispered the word. Auditions for *A Woman in Love* were going to be held just after the Easter production, according to Marti. And Vincent Cason, the director, had specifically asked about Tangie for the lead. Though flattered, the idea of going back home to the Big Apple scared her senseless. On the other hand, she didn't want to miss God. Was He wooing her back to finish what He'd started four years ago, perhaps?

Minutes later, a customer arrived—a woman ordering a wedding cake. Thankfully, Tangie had some experience with cakes. Her mom made ice cream cakes for brides all the time. How different could a baked cake be? She located Penny's sample book and walked the young woman—who introduced herself as Brenna—through the process.

"I've already talked to Penny about the size and style," Brenna explained. "We settled on a four-tier with cream cheese frosting. But I wasn't sure about my wedding colors until this week."

"Sounds like I'll need some specifics about the wedding, then," Tangie said, reaching for a tablet.

"The wedding is on April 14," Brenna responded with a smile. "I've waited for years for Mr. Right, and now that I've found him, I can't stand waiting three months. Is that silly?"

"Doesn't sound silly at all. What's the point in a long engagement when you've done nothing but wait up till then?" She scribbled the date on the notepad and then looked up at Brenna. "Where is the wedding taking place?"

"Harmony Community Church."

"Oh, that's my church," Tangie said.

"Really? I don't recognize you. But then again, that church is growing like wildfire, so it's getting harder to recognize everyone."

"I'm new. They just hired me to direct the children's plays."

"Oh, wait. . ." Brenna looked at her with renewed interest. "Is your name Tangie or something like that?"

"Yes."

Brenna nodded. "I was working in the nursery the week you were introduced, but my son Cody told me all about you. He's scared to death I'm going to make him be in the next play. He, um. . .well, he didn't have the best time in the last one."

"Ah." So this was Cody's mom. "Well, I think I can safely say this one will be more fun." She hoped.

"It's hard, being a single mom and trying to keep your son interested in things going on at church." Brenna's words were followed by a dramatic sigh. "I have to practically wrestle with him just to get him through the kids' church door on Sunday mornings. I'll be so glad when Phil and I get married. He's going to be a great dad for Cody."

Tangie paused to think about the little boy. Gran-Gran had mentioned he came from a single-parent home, but didn't say anything about an upcoming wedding. Then again, maybe she didn't know.

Nah. Scratch that. In Harmony, pretty much everyone knew everyone else's business. And then some.

"Let's talk more about the cake," Tangie said, offering Brenna a seat. "What are your wedding colors and what type of flowers will you carry?"

"The bridesmaids' dresses are blue and the flowers are coral and white. Lilies. I know Penny can make the lilies because I've seen her sugar-work in the past."

"Wonderful. I'll just write this down and give it to her when she gets back," Tangie explained. "If she has any questions, I'm sure she'll call. And I'll let her take care of getting your deposit."

"Oh, no bother." Brenna reached into her purse for her checkbook. "We've already talked through this part. I'm leaving a hundred dollar deposit today and will pay the rest the week before the wedding."

They wrapped up their meeting and Brenna rose to leave. Afterward, Tangie went to work in the back room, tidying things up. Looked like Penny hadn't stayed on top of that. Likely her workload was too great.

About three hours later Penny returned, looking a bit winded. "Sorry, hon. But it's gonna be like this till my treatments end."

"Your treatments?"

"Forgot to mention that part, didn't I? I drive over to Trenton for chemo two days a week. Breast cancer. I was just diagnosed about two months ago."

"Oh, Penny. I'm so sorry." Tangie shook her head. "You should have told me."

With the wave of a hand, Penny went back to work. "I'm trying not to let it consume me. But I must warn you"—she began to look a little pale—"that sometimes my stomach doesn't handle the chemo very well."

At that, she sprinted to the back room. Tangie followed along behind her, stopping at the restroom door. "You okay in there?" she called out.

"Mm-hmm." Penny groaned. "Nothing I haven't been through before." After a pause, she hollered, "Would you mind putting another batch of sugar cookies in the oven? The after-school crowd will be here in less than an hour, and I'm not ready for them. The cookie dough is already rolled into balls in the walk-in refrigerator. Just put a dozen on each tray. Bake them for ten minutes."

"Of course." Tangie carried on with her work, silently ushering up a prayer for Penny. Looked like she needed all the prayers she could get.

❧

Gregg sat at his desk, reading over the script Tangie had e-mailed. Though different from anything he would have ever chosen, he had to admit the story line was clever, and probably something the kids would really get into. He would play along, for the sake of time—and in the spirit of cooperation. But as for whether or not he would enjoy it? That was another thing altogether.

He exhaled, releasing some of the tension of the day. In some ways, it felt like things were spinning out of control. Not that he ever had any control, really. But the illusion of having any was quickly fading. Gregg couldn't control the things his mother was going through. He couldn't control things with Ashley, who'd just informed him she might give her relationship with her old boyfriend another try. And he certainly couldn't control the madness surrounding Tangie Carini and the kids' musical.

"Lord, what are you trying to show me here?"

As if in response, Gregg's gaze shifted up to the plaque on the wall, one the choir members had given him for his last birthday. He smiled as he read the familiar scripture: FINALLY, ALL OF YOU, LIVE IN HARMONY WITH ONE ANOTHER. 1 PET. 3:8. He smiled as he thought about the irony. *Live in harmony*.

Sometimes it was easier living in the *town* than living in the sort of harmonious state the scripture referred to. Still, he'd give it his best shot. God was calling him to no less.

With a renewed sense of purpose, Gregg turned back to his work.

nine

On the following Sunday afternoon, Tangie stood in the fellowship hall, preparing herself for the auditions. She placed tidy stacks of audition forms on the table, alongside freshly sharpened pencils and bottles of water for the directors. Brittany had agreed to help, thank goodness. And Gregg would take care of the vocal auditions. Yes, everything was coming together quite nicely. Now, if only they could find the right kids for each role, then all would be well.

"Ready for the big day?"

She turned as she heard Gregg's voice. "Hey. Glad you're here. I want to run this form by you before the kids arrive."

"What form?" Gregg drew close and glanced at the papers in her hand. "What have you got there?"

"Oh, it's an audition form, designed especially for today. Look." She held one up for his inspection. "See this section at the top? Brittany and I will use this section for the drama auditions. There's a column for characterization—does the child really look and act the part? Then there's another for inflection, another for expression, and another for volume. It's pretty straightforward. You'll see a spot at the top where the child fills out his or her name, age, and prior experience on the stage."

"Ah ha." He seemed to be scrutinizing the page.

"I've created a separate section at the bottom for the vocal auditions," Tangie added, pointing. "It gives you a place to comment on things like pitch, projection, harmonization skills, tone, and so forth."

He pursed his lips, then said, "Good idea. We could've used something like that when we auditioned the kids at Christmastime."

His words of affirmation warmed Tangie's heart. "Did you use some sort of form for the Christmas play?"

"Nope. The whole thing was organized chaos. We were all in the room at the same time."

"That's your first problem." Tangie laughed. "It's always better to hold auditions in a private setting, one at a time. Helps the child relax and that way they can't copy from one another." Tangie spoke from experience. She'd been through too many open auditions where candidates tripped all over themselves to one-up the people who'd gone before them. But none of that here. No sir.

"I never thought of doing it this way." Gregg shook his head. "But I'm always open to ideas. When we did the last auditions, it literally took all day. Each child wanted to audition for half a dozen parts. And then there were the would-be soloists." He groaned. "You wouldn't believe how many times I had to listen to "Silent Night." Trust me, it wasn't a silent night. Chaotic, yes. Silent, no." He offered up a winsome smile and for the first time, she saw a glimmer of hope.

"Well, here's something I've learned from other shows I've been in," Tangie said. "It's best to get the music auditions over with first. That way, you can mark on the form if you think the child can handle a lead role before I ever let him or her read for a part. Then I'll know which roles they can and can't be considered for."

"Sounds like a good plan. I'll have your grandmother bring the child's form to you after the vocal audition. That way the kids can't see what we're doing."

Tangie nodded. "Oh, one more thing. . ." She handed him a stack of the papers. "Some of the kids probably won't be interested in auditioning for vocal solos, so they can come straight to the drama audition. I've got plenty of roles to go around, and many of them aren't singing roles."

"I'd still like all of the children to be in the choir, though," he added. "We need as many voices as we can get."

"Well, let's talk about that afterward, okay?" She gave him a pensive look. "Not every child is an actor, but not every child is a vocalist, either. Some aren't crazy about singing in a group. So, why don't we pray about that?"

For a moment, he looked as if he might refute her. Then, just as quickly, he nodded. "I'm sure the sanctuary is about to burst at the seams with kids by now. Let's get in there and give our instructions. Then we'll start."

"Before we do, would you mind if we prayed about this?"

"Of course not."

As a matter of habit, Tangie reached to take his hand. She bowed her head and ushered up a passionate prayer that the Lord's will would be done in these auditions—that exactly the right child would get each part.

"And, Lord," she continued, "if there's a child here who hasn't come to know You, may this be the production that leads him or her to You. And for those who do know You, Father, please use these next few weeks to stir up the gifts You've placed in each boy and girl. Help develop them into the person they will one day be."

"And, Lord," Gregg threw in, "we ask for Your will regarding the ones who don't fit in. Show us what to do with the ones who are, well, difficult."

They closed out the prayer with a quick "Amen," and Gregg's smile warmed Tangie's heart. "Thanks for suggesting that. I always pray with the kids before every practice, but I never thought about actually praying for the audition process before the fact."

"It always helps." She shrugged. "And besides, if we ask God to be at the center of it, then—when we're in the throes of rehearsing and things are getting rough—we can be sure that we've really chosen the right people for the job. We won't be tempted to toss the baby out with the bath water."

He quirked a brow and she laughed.

"I just mean we won't be tempted to take the part away from

him—or her—and give it to someone else. If we pray about this ahead of time, then we're confident that God has special plans for that particular child in that role. See what I mean?"

"Yes." He nodded. "But I never really thought about it like that before. I guess I never saw this whole process as being terribly spiritual. It's just a kids' play."

"Oh no." She shook her head. "It's not just a kids' play. It's so much more than that." Tangie was tempted to dive into a lengthy discussion, but one glance at her watch served as a reminder that dozens of kids waited in the sanctuary.

"After you," she said, pointing.

He turned her way one last time, a curious expression on his face. "Before we start, I just have one question."

"Sure. What's up?"

"I just need to know. . .what *are* you wearing?" He pointed to her beret, which she pulled off and gripped with a smile.

"Ah. My cap. I always wear it on audition day. It puts me in a theatrical frame of mind."

"Mm-hmm." He chuckled, and they headed off together to face the energetic mob.

❧

Gregg looked up as Margaret Sanderson entered the choir room, a confident smile lighting her cherub-like face. She wore her hair in tight ringlets, and her dress—an over-the-top frills number—convinced him she was here to do business.

"Good to see you, Margaret. Are you ready to audition for us?" Gregg asked, trying to remain positive.

Margaret nodded. "Oh, I am. And my mother says I should tell you that I'm interested in trying out for the leading role."

"Yes, but would you be willing to take any role if you don't get a lead?" It was a fair question, one Gregg planned to ask every child who auditioned.

Margaret paused and bit her lip. After a second, she said, "I, well, I guess. But my mom says I have the best voice in the whole church."

"Ah." Gregg stifled a laugh and looked down at his papers. "You do have a nice singing voice," he said, "But, of course, we have to listen to everyone before making our decision."

He took a seat at his piano and began to play the introduction to "Amazing Grace," the song he'd instructed all of the children to prepare in advance.

Margaret interrupted him, setting a piece of music down in front of him. "I've brought my own audition music. I would prefer to sing *it*—if you don't mind. My mother says it showcases my voice." She belted out "The Lullaby of Broadway," which to her credit, did sound pretty good.

Gregg covered her form with high marks, then handed it to Tangie's grandmother, who had agreed to run interference between the music department and the drama department.

Next Cody arrived. His mother practically pushed him in the door. "Go on in, son. You can do this."

"But I don't want to!" He groaned, then eased his way toward the piano.

"Lord, give me strength," Gregg whispered. "This one tries my patience." He turned to the youngster with a smile. "Cody, let's hear a couple lines of 'Amazing Grace.'"

The boy groaned. "Remember we did this last time? I stink. Why do I have to do it again?"

Gregg began to play. "Well, you've had some musical experience since then. Maybe there's been some improvement."

Cody began to sing, just not exactly in the key Gregg happened to be playing at the moment. Looked like nothing had changed, after all. After just a few notes, Cody stopped and crossed his arms at his chest. "See what I mean? I stink."

"Well, I understand Miss Tangie has some drama roles that don't require singing this time around," Gregg said. "So why don't you head on over to the fellowship hall and audition for her?"

"Really? I don't have to sing?"

"That's right."

When Gregg nodded, the youngster looked at him as if he'd just been offered an eleventh hour stay. He sprinted out of the door with more exaggerated energy.

The next child in the room was Annabelle Lawrence. She was a sweet thing—probably eight or so—but a little on the shy side. Understandable, since her family was new to the church. As Gregg listened to her sing, he was pleasantly surprised. Nice voice. Very nice. "Have you done any performing, Annabelle?"

She shook her head and spoke in a soft voice. "No, but I think I would like it."

He filled out her form, smiling. Over the two and a half hours, the kids came and went from the room. Gregg heard those who could sing, and those who couldn't. A couple of them insisted upon rapping their audition and one sang "Amazing Grace" in Spanish. In all, the variety was pretty interesting. His favorite was a little boy named Joey who proclaimed, "I want to sing. . .real bad!" Unfortunately his audition proved that he could. Sing bad, that was.

By the time the afternoon ended, Gregg had a much clearer picture of where they stood. Thankfully, there were some great singers in the bunch. Looked like the Easter production might just turn out okay, after all.

🍃

Tangie scribbled note after note as the children came and went from her room. Some were better than others, naturally, but a few were absolutely darling. And, as they read the lines from the play she'd written, the words absolutely sprang to life. There was something so satisfying about hearing her words acted out.

Not that all of the kids were actors. No, a few would be better served in smaller roles, to be sure. And a couple of the ones who could act—though good—struggled with a little too much confidence. There would be plenty of time to work on that.

By the time the last child left, things were looking a little clearer. Yes, Tangie could almost see which child would fit which part. Now all she had to do was convince Gregg. Then. . . let the show begin!

ten

After the auditions ended, Tangie sat with papers in hand, going over every note. Looked like this was going to be easier than she'd first thought. Some of the kids were obvious; others, not so much.

She laughed as she read some of the forms. Under PRIOR EXPERIENCE, one little boy had written *I sing in the shower*. One of the girls had scribbled the words, *Broadway, Here I Come!*

Ah, yes. Margaret Sanderson. Tangie sighed as she looked at the youngster's resume, complete with headshot. "She really wants the lead role something awful."

Awful being the key word. The little darling had pretty much insisted she get the part. That didn't sit well with Tangie.

She flipped through the forms until she found one for a little girl named Annabelle. Though Annabelle had no prior experience, there was something about her that had captivated Tangie right away. Her sweet expression as she read the lines. Her genuine emotion as she took on the character of the littlest sheep. Sure, she needed a bit of work. Maybe more than a bit. But Tangie always rooted for the underdog. Nothing new there. And from Gregg's notes, she could tell the child had a wonderful singing voice.

Tangie yawned and looked at Brittany, who laughed.

"Had enough fun for one day?" the teen asked.

"Mm-hmm. Don't think I could do this for a living." Tangie paused a moment, then added, "Oh, yeah. I already do." A grin followed.

"I'm still hoping you'll think about that community theater

idea," Brittany said, her brow wrinkling as she spoke.

Tangie sighed, not wanting to burst the teen's bubble. How could she tell her she was thinking of leaving Harmony in April? Today wasn't the day.

Tangie turned her attention back to the audition forms, placing them in three stacks: To be considered for a lead. To be considered for a smaller role. To be dealt with. Thankfully, the "To be dealt with" pile was the smallest of the three. Still, it contained Cody's form. Poor guy couldn't sing or act, at least from what she could tell. "Lord," she whispered, "show us where to place him. I don't want to put him—or us—through any more agony than necessary."

As she pondered the possibilities, Gregg entered the room, a look of exhaustion on his face.

"How did the vocal auditions go?" she asked. "Or is that a silly question?"

He shrugged. "Not too bad, actually. Things were a lot smoother with the forms you created. Still, if I have to hear 'Amazing Grace' one more time. . ." He laughed. "I just don't know if I can take it."

"Any ideas about lead roles?" Tangie asked, preparing herself to show Gregg the completed audition forms. "Because I have so many thoughts rolling through my head right now." She picked up the first stack of papers, ready to dive in.

He looked at the papers and grinned. "I have a few ideas, but let me ask you a question first."

"Sure."

"Did you really stack those forms like that, or did someone else do it?"

"I did it." She shrugged. "I'm usually right-brained, but not when it comes to something like this. When it comes to the important stuff, I have all my ducks in a row." She paused a moment, then added, "Why do you ask?"

He shrugged. "It's just that I'm like that. . .pretty much all the time. You should see the stacks of mail at my place." A boyish grin lit his face. He paused a moment, then asked, "Are you hungry?"

"Starved." Tangie nodded, hoping her grumbling stomach wouldn't show him just how hungry she was.

"Want to go to the diner for some food? It's open late and we can eat while we talk. I'll drive, if it's okay with you."

"Sounds amazing."

"As in '*Amazing* Grace'?"

Tangie laughed.

Brittany spoke up, interrupting their conversation. "Tangie, I told my mom I'd be home right after auditions. I've got school tomorrow."

"Thank you so much for your help." Tangie smiled at the exuberant teen. "Don't think I could've done it without you."

"Sure you could've." Brittany grinned. "But I'm glad you didn't choose to."

Ten minutes later, amid steaming cups of coffee and tea, Tangie spread the audition forms across the table. "Let's start with the ones who can sing."

"Sure. We have quite a few in that category." Gregg took a drink of his coffee, thumbing through the forms. "Now, Margaret Sanderson will play the lead, right? She's by far our best singer."

Tangie bit her tongue, willing herself not to knee-jerk. This was bound to be a source of contention.

"She's our strongest vocalist *and* has a lot of experience." Gregg looked over her form, nodding as he read the comments. "And she's tiny enough to play the role of the little sheep, don't you think?"

"Yes, she's the right size, but. . .well, experience isn't always the only thing to consider."

"What do you mean?" He looked up from the form, a puzzled expression on his face.

Tangie leaned her elbows onto the table and stared at Gregg. "Don't you think she's a little. . .well. . .stuck-up?"

"Hmm." He shrugged. "*Stuck-up* might not be the words I would've come up with. When you're really good at something, sometimes you come across as overly confident."

"She's overly confident, all right. She pretty much told me I was giving her the lead in the show. And you should hear what her mother's been saying to people."

Gregg laughed. "She's used to getting her way. I've seen that side of her before."

Tangie opted to change gears. "What about Annabelle? How did she do in the vocal audition?"

"Annabelle Lawrence? The new girl?" He shuffled through his papers until he found the right one. "Oh, right. She had a nice voice for someone with no experience. Pitch was pretty good. Nice tone. But she's not a strong performer."

"What do you mean?" Tangie felt more than a little rankled at that comment. "She did a great job in the drama auditions."

"Really? Hmm." Gregg shrugged. "Well, maybe you can give her a small part or something. And she can always sing in the choir."

"I don't think you're hearing me," Tangie said, feeling her temper mount. "If Annabelle can sing, I'd like to consider her for the lead role."

Gregg paled, then took another swig of his coffee. "Lead role? Are. . .are you serious?"

"Of course." Tangie stood her ground. "Why not?"

He shook his head and placed his cup back on the table. "Look, I already botched up the Christmas play. I have a lot to prove with this one. My best shot at pulling this off is using kids who are seasoned. Talented."

"So, this is about making you look good?" Tangie quirked a brow. Looked like he was trying to prove something here, but at whose expense? The kids?

He groaned and shook his head. "Maybe I put too much emphasis on that part. But I feel like I need to redeem myself after what happened before."

"But at whose expense?" She stared him down, curious how he would respond.

"Whose expense?" Gregg looked flustered. "What do you mean?"

"I mean, Margaret Sanderson is at a crossroads. She's a little diva and she needs to understand that she won't always be the one in the lead role. Sometimes the underdog needs a chance."

At once, Tangie's hands began to tremble. Something about the word *underdog* sent a shiver down her spine. How often had she been in that position over the years? Too many to count. Take that last play, for example. The one where she'd been promised the lead, but had had to settle for a bit part in the chorus. She'd handled it as well as could be expected, but when would she get her turn? When would she take center stage?

Tangie sighed, then turned her attention back to the forms. This time she could actually control who landed in which spot. And she would make sure she didn't botch it up.

❧

Gregg stared across the table at Tangie, confused by her words. "Tell me what you're really thinking here, Tangie. How many grown-up Margaret Sandersons have you had to work with?"

"W–what do you mean?"

"I mean, maybe you're sympathetic toward Annabelle because you can relate to her. That's my guess, anyway. How many times did you try for the lead role and someone like Margaret got it instead?"

Ouch. "A million?" Tangie responded, after absorbing the sting of his question. "But I got over it."

"I'm not so sure you did. I think maybe you're still holding a grudge against leading ladies and want to prove a point. So, you're going to use Margaret to do it. If you prevent her from getting the lead, it will be payback to all of those leading ladies who got the parts you felt you deserved over the years."

Tangie's face paled. "Nothing could be further from the truth," she argued. "It's just that the character of the baby ewe is a really sweet personality and Annabelle can pull that off. Margaret couldn't pull off sweet without a significant amount of work."

"But I want her in the lead because she's the strongest vocalist." Gregg stood his ground on this one. If they put anyone other than Margaret in the role, it would double his workload.

"I have to disagree." The creases between Tangie's brows deepened and she leaned back against her seat, arms tightly crossed.

Gregg stared at her, unsure of what to say next. Why was she going to such lengths to challenge him on this? Margaret was the better singer. Who cared if she had a little attitude problem? They could work with her and she would get over it. Right? Yes, this production would surely give them the platform they needed to further develop her talents while giving her some gentle life lessons along the way.

Tangie began to argue for Annabelle, but Gregg had a hard time staying focused. Thankfully, the waitress showed up to take their order. That gave him a two-minute reprieve. After she left, Tangie dove right back in. They were able to cast everyone in the show—except Margaret and Annabelle. This was an easy one, to his way of thinking. Give Annabelle a smaller part and let Margaret take the lead.

Unfortunately, Tangie refused to bend.

They finished the meal in strained silence. Afterward, Gregg led the way to his car. He'd never had someone get him quite as riled up as he felt right now. As he opened the car door for Tangie, he paused to tell her one more thing. "It's obvious we're two very different people with two very different ways of looking at things."

"What are you saying? That I'm too different for this church? For this town?"

He paused, not knowing how to respond. "I just think we need to pick our battles, Tangie. Some mountains aren't worth dying on."

She stared at him, her big brown eyes screaming out her frustration. "We both need to go home and sleep on this," she suggested. "I'm too tired to make much sense out of things tonight. And besides, we're meeting tomorrow afternoon at the church to finalize things, right? Let's just drop it for now."

"But I don't want to leave it hanging in midair till then." Gregg shook his head. "I want to understand why you're being so stubborn about this. What are you thinking, anyway?"

"I'm thinking this will be a good time to teach Margaret a couple of life lessons. The top dog doesn't always get the bone, Gregg."

"She's a kid, not a golden retriever," he responded.

Back and forth they went, arguing about who should—or shouldn't—play the various roles in the play. All the while, Gregg felt more and more foolish about the words coming out of his mouth. In fact, at one point, he found himself unable to focus on anything other than the pain on her beautiful face and guilt over the fact that he'd put it there.

Tangie's hands began to tremble—likely from the anger— and he reached to take them, suddenly very ashamed of himself for getting her so worked up.

With hands clasped, she stared at him, silence rising up between them. Except for the sound of Gregg's heartbeat, which he imagined she must be able to hear as clearly as he did, everything grew silent.

Then, like a man possessed, Gregg did the unthinkable.

He kissed her.

eleven

On the morning after auditions, Tangie wandered the house in a daze. *He kissed me. He. Kissed. Me.*

"But, why?" She'd done nothing to encourage it, right?

Okay, there had been that one moment when she'd paused from her righteous tirade, captivated by his bright blue eyes. . . eyes that had held her attention a microsecond longer than they should have, perhaps. But had that been enough to cause such a reaction from him? Clearly not. And wasn't he interested in Ashley, anyway? Why would he be so fickle as to kiss the wrong woman?

Hmm. She couldn't exactly accuse others of being fickle when she had flitted from relationship to relationship, could she?

"Still. . ." Tangie paced the living room, her thoughts reeling. "What in the world is wrong with him?"

"Wrong with who?" Gramps asked. "Or would it be whom? I never could get that straight."

"Oh, I. . ." Tangie shook her head, unable to respond. She raked her fingers through her hair. "Never mind."

"What has Gregg done now?" Gramps asked, putting up his fists in mock preparation for a boxing match. "If he's hurt your feelings or gotten you worked up over something, I'll take him down. Just watch and see. I'm not too old to do it."

Tangie chuckled and then released an exaggerated sigh. "Gramps, there are some things about men I will never understand. Not if I live to be a hundred."

"I feel the same way about women, to be honest," he said, and then laughed. "And I'm three-quarters of my way to a hundred, so I don't have a lot of time left to figure it all out. So I guess that makes us even. We're both equally confused."

Yes, confused. That was the word, all right. Everything about the past couple of weeks confused her. Driving in the dead of winter to a town she hardly knew. Taking a job at a church where she didn't fit in. Working with a man who. . .

Whose eyes were the color of a Monet sky. Whose voice sounded like a heavenly choir. When he wasn't chewing her out or accusing her of being too outlandish.

She turned to Gramps with a strained smile, determined not to let him see any more of her frustration or her sudden interest in the music pastor. He'd seen enough already. "Are you hungry? We could go to the bakery." Tangie reached for her keys and then grabbed her coat from the hook in the front hall. "My treat."

"Sweet Harmony? I'd love to!" His eyes lit up. "I'm always up for an éclair or one of those bear claw things. Or both. Just don't tell your grandmother when she gets back from her nibble and dribble group."

"Nibble and dribble?" Tangie turned to him, confused.

He shrugged. "You know. That ladies' tea she goes to every month. It's just an excuse for a bunch of women to sit around and sip tea and nibble on microscopic cookies and cakes and dribble chatter all over one another. Never could figure out the appeal. I'd rather have the real thing from Sweet Harmony. Now there's some sugar you can sink your teeth into."

Tangie laughed. "Ah, I see. Well, I'm in the mood for something over the top, too. But you'll have to hide all of the evidence if you don't want Gran-Gran to know."

"Good idea. I'll bring some chewing gum with me. That'll get rid of the sugar breath and throw your grandmother off track."

"You sound like you've done this before."

He gave her a wink. "Let's hit the road, girlie."

"I'm ready when you are."

All the way, she forced the conversation away from Gregg

Burke and toward anything and everything that might cause distraction.

Her thoughts kept drifting back to the auditions. The kids expected the cast list to be posted on Wednesday evening before service. How could they post it if she and Gregg couldn't even come to an agreement? When they met together this afternoon, they would come up with a logical plan. Surely the man could be reasoned with. Right?

Every time she thought about spending time with him, Tangie's thoughts reeled back to that tempestuous kiss. Sure, she'd been kissed before, but never by a man so upset. Gregg had been downright mad at her just seconds before he planted that kiss on her unsuspecting lips. She hadn't seen either coming—the anger or the startling smooch. And both had left her reeling, though for completely different reasons. She didn't know if she wanted to punch his lights out or melt in his arms.

The former certainly held more appeal than the latter, at least at the moment.

Tangie did her best to focus on the road, happy to finally arrive at the bakery. With Gramps leading the way, she entered the shop.

"Hey, Penny," Gramps called out.

"Well, Herbert, it's not Sunday," Penny responded, her brows rising in surprise. "What brings you to the shop today?"

"This granddaughter of mine. She talked me into it. Tangie's got sugar in her veins. It's from all those years working at the candy shop in Atlantic City."

"She's working for me now, you know," Penny said. "And we're talking about adding candies to Sweet Harmony."

"Ya don't say." His eyes lit up.

"Yes. And by the way, Tangie can take home leftovers any afternoon when we close. So, between you and me, you don't have to pay for your sweets anymore. Except on Sundays."

"Are you serious?" From the look on Gramps' face, he might as well have won the lottery. He turned in Tangie's direction.

"Well, why didn't you tell me?"

She shrugged. "I didn't know. But we'd better take it easy with the sweets. Don't want your blood sugars to peak."

"My blood sugars are perfect," he explained. Turning to Penny, he said, "So I'll have a bear claw, an éclair, and a half dozen donut holes for good measure."

"Sure you don't want a kolache to go along with that?" Penny asked.

"Why not?" He shrugged. "Tangie's paying."

"Penny might have to mortage the business to cover that order," she said with a laugh. When his eyes narrowed in concern, she added, "But that's okay. You're worth it, Gramps. You're worth it."

❧

On Monday around noon, Gregg slipped away from the office to grab a bite to eat at home. After taking a few bites of his sandwich, he paced his living room, thinking back over the events of the past twenty-four hours.

He still couldn't get over the fact that Tangie didn't want to cast Margaret Sanderson in the lead role. Didn't make a lick of sense to him. Then again, women didn't make a lick of sense to him.

On the other hand, his *own* actions didn't make sense, either.

Had he really kissed Tangie? Right there, in the diner parking lot for the whole town of Harmony to see? Why? What had prompted such irrational behavior on his part? Something about her had reeled him in. *What is my problem lately? Why is everything upside down in my life all of a sudden?*

Something about that crazy, unpredictable girl had gotten to him. And it frustrated him to no end. Gregg took a seat at the piano. . .the place where he always worked out his troubles. Somehow, pounding the black and white keys brought a sense of release. And there was something about turning his troubles into beautiful melodies that lifted his spirits. No, he certainly couldn't stay upset for long with music pouring from his fingertips, could he?

Gregg was halfway into a worship medley when the doorbell rang. He answered the door, stunned to see his younger brother.

"Josh?" Gregg swung the door back and grinned. "You should tell a person when you're coming for a visit."

"Why?" Josh shook off the snow and shivered in an exaggerated sort of way. "It's always so much more fun when I just show up. Besides, you know I don't stay in one place very long. I always end up back here, in Harmony."

"Yes, but you're back sooner than usual this time. What happened in New York?"

Josh shrugged as he eased his way through the front door. "Oh, you know. A little of this, a little of that. More this than that."

"Mm-hmm. What's her name?"

After a moment's pause, Josh offered up a dramatic sigh. "Julia."

"She broke your heart?"

"No, but her boyfriend almost broke my nose." Josh grinned, then rubbed his nose, making a funny face.

"You've got to get past this thing where you jump from girl to girl," Gregg said. "It's not healthy—for you or the girls."

"Might work for you to dedicate yourself to one at a time, but I'm not wired that way." Josh shrugged. "Got anything to eat in that refrigerator of yours?"

"Sure. Help yourself." Gregg sat back down at the piano and continued to play. A few minutes later, Josh showed up in the living room with a sandwich in hand. "That's a great piece you're playing. What do you call that?"

Gregg looked up from the piano and shook his head. "Not sure yet. I'm just making it up as I go along."

"No way." Josh smiled. "I thought it was a real song."

"It will be." Gregg allowed a few more notes to trip from

his fingertips, then turned around on the piano bench to face his younger brother. They hadn't seen each other in months. And knowing Josh, he wouldn't be here for long.

Gregg spent the next hour talking to his brother—catching up on the time they'd been apart.

"I've been talking to Mom at least once a week," Josh said. "So, I know everything that's going on. She's doing better than I thought she would."

"Yes. Does she know you're back?"

"Yeah. I stopped by the shop just now. She seems to be doing okay. I hear she's hired someone to help."

"Yes. Someone I know pretty well, actually. A girl from church."

Josh's brows elevated. "Oh?"

"She's not someone you would be interested in. She's a little on the wacky side."

"I like wacky. You're the one who picks the straight arrows. Not me."

Gregg changed the direction of the conversation right away, realizing he and Josh were now talking about two completely different things. "I'm glad you're back. Mom really needs us right now."

"I know." Josh nodded. "I might be a wanderer, but even I know when it's time to head home for a while."

"Good." Gregg released a sigh, feeling some of his anxieties lift. "Well, I'm glad you're home. He glanced at the clock on the wall, rising to his feet as he realized the time. "I hate to cut this short, but I've got a meeting at the church in twenty minutes."

"Oh? Should I tag along?"

Gregg shrugged. "A couple of us are meeting in the choir room to talk about the Easter production. Pretty boring stuff, unless you're involved."

"Any beautiful females in the mix?"

Gregg hesitated to answer, knowing his brother's penchant

for pretty women. "Oh, you know. Just church ladies." That was only a slight exaggeration. Tangie did go to the church after all, and she was a lady.

"Church ladies." Josh laughed. "Sounds intriguing. Thanks for the invitation. I'd be happy to."

twelve

Tangie looked up from her notes as Gregg and the handsome stranger entered the choir room.

Her heart began to flutter as she turned her attention to Gregg. *Lord, help me through this. I don't know if I'm ever going to be able to look him in the eye again after what happened last night.* If she closed her eyes, she could relive the moment over and over again. Why, oh why, hadn't she pulled away when he leaned in to kiss her? Why had she lingered in his arms, enjoying the unexpected surprise of the moment?

Because she was a fickle girl who fell in love more often than she changed her hair color. And that was pretty often.

As Gregg made introductions, her gaze lingered on Josh. So, this was Gregg's brother. They resembled each other in many ways, but there was something different about Josh. He was younger, sure. And trendier. He certainly wore the name-brand clothes with confidence. The look of assurance—or was that cockiness?—set him apart from Gregg in many ways.

"So, where do you hail from?" she asked Josh as he took the seat across from her.

"Manhattan."

That certainly got Tangie's attention. She turned to him, stunned. "You're kidding. Where do you live in Manhattan?"

"East end. I love the city life. Always seems strange, coming back to Harmony."

"Oh, I know. Tell me about it."

Within seconds the two of them were engaged in a full-on conversation. Tangie could hardly believe it. Finally! Someone who shared her enthusiasm for big city life.

"What do you do for a living?" she asked.

"I'm a reporter. Did some work for the *Times*, but that's a tough gig. A couple of the local papers bought my pieces, but the competition in the city is fierce. So, I'm back in Harmony."

"As always." Gregg walked over to the coffee maker and switched it on.

"Yeah." Josh shrugged. "I usually come back home when things slow down. The editor at the *Gazette* always gives me my old job back."

"Oh? They let you come and go like that?"

"He's a great guy." Josh sighed and leaned back against the seat. "Not that there's ever much news in this town. But I can always write stories on Mr. Clark's rheumatism and Mrs. Miller's liver condition." He laughed. "Not quite the same buzz as New York City, but it pays the light bill."

"Oh, I understand. I love the city. And you're right. . .it's filled with stories." Tangie dove into a passionate speech about her favorite places to go in Manhattan and before long, she and Josh were in a heated debate over their favorite—and least favorite—restaurants.

"What did you do in New York, anyway?" he asked.

"Tangie's a Broadway star," Gregg interjected.

That certainly caught Tangie's attention. She'd never heard him describe her in such a way. Glancing at Gregg, she tried to figure out if his words were meant to be flattering or sarcastic. The expression on his face wasn't clear.

"Really?" Josh looked at her with an admiring smile. "You're an actress?"

"Well, technically, I only did a couple of bit parts on Broadway. Most of my work was in theaters a few blocks away. But I did have a few secondary roles that got written up in the paper."

"Which paper?"

"The *Times*. It was a review of *Happily Never After*. I played the role of Nadine, the embittered ex-girlfriend."

"Wait, I saw that show. It shut down after just a couple of weeks, right?"

Tangie felt her cheeks warm. She looked at Gregg, wondering what he would make of this news.

"Yes. But that's okay. It wasn't one of my favorites. We never found our audience."

"Lost 'em, eh?" He laughed. "Happens to shows all the time. I just hate it for the sake of those involved. And I especially hated writing some of those reviews. It's always tough to crush people."

"Wait. . ." She paused, looking at him intently. "You said you wrote for the paper, but you didn't mention you were a reviewer."

"I'm not. . .technically." He laughed. "But whenever the other reviewers were too busy, I'd fill in. I got stuck with a lot of off-off-Broadway shows and some of them were, well, pretty rank."

"Mm-hmm." A shiver ran down Tangie's spine. Before long, he might start naming some of those not-so-great shows.

"How does a reviewer receive his training, anyway?" she asked. "On the stage or off?"

"Both." Josh shrugged. "In my case, anyway."

"Oh, he's got a lot of experience." Gregg approached the table with a cup of coffee in his hands. "Josh here is quite the actor. He's been in plays since we were kids."

"Really." Tangie scrutinized him. "We need someone to play the role of the shepherd in our Easter production. Would you be interested in auditioning?"

Josh turned her way with a smile. "Now that's a proposition I just might have to consider."

ॐ

Gregg could have kicked himself the minute he heard Tangie's question. Putting on this Easter production was going to be tough enough. Factoring Josh into the equation would only complicate things further.

"Josh is too—" He was going to say *busy*, when his brother interrupted him.

"I'd love to."

"It's for the church," Gregg explained. "And I'm not sure you're the best person for the job."

"Why not?" Josh gave him a pensive look. "You said you needed an actor. I'm here. What else is there to know?"

Gregg bit his tongue. Literally. Josh's walk with the Lord wasn't as strong as it once was. In fact, Gregg couldn't be sure where his brother was in his spiritual journey. In order to play the lead—the character of the Good Shepherd—the actor should, at the very least, understand God's heart toward His children. Right?

Gregg sighed, unsure of where to take this conversation. He'd have to get Tangie alone and explain all of this to her. However, from the enthusiastic look on her face, persuading her might not be as easy as he hoped.

Lord, show me what to do here. If You're trying to nudge my brother back home—to You—I don't want to get in the way.

"Okay, everyone." Tangie's words interrupted his thoughts. "Aren't we here to cast a show? Let's get to it."

With a sigh, Gregg turned his attention to the matter at hand.

 ❧

Tangie arrived home from the meeting, her thoughts going a hundred different directions. Gregg had finally agreed that Annabelle could play the lead, but he wasn't happy about it. Tangie couldn't help but think Gregg was put off by her ideas, across the board. Of course, he just seemed "off" today, anyway. That much was obvious when he knocked over her cup of tea, spilling it all over the table. She could also tell the stuff about his brother being in the play bothered him. . .but why? Sure, Josh was a schmoozer. She knew his type. But Gregg was acting almost. . .jealous. Surely he didn't think Tangie would be interested in Josh.

No, guys like Josh were too familiar. They came and went through your life. Besides, she and Josh had far too much in common. What would be the fun in that?

As she entered the house, Tangie made her way into the kitchen to grab a soda and a snack. With all of the goodies from the bakery on hand, she felt sure she'd end up packing on the pounds before long. Especially if she couldn't get her emotions under control. Still, she couldn't stop thinking about Gregg. About that kiss. Was it keeping him preoccupied today, as well? She hadn't been able to tell while they were together. Maybe he was a better actor than she thought. Or maybe... She sighed. Maybe he regretted what he'd done.

As Tangie left the kitchen, a soda in one hand and two peanut butter cookies in the other, she ran into Gran-Gran in the hallway.

"Well, there you are. That meeting went longer than you expected." Her grandmother gave her an odd look. "Everything okay?"

"Yeah." She shrugged. "It took us awhile to figure out which child should play which part, and we didn't all agree, even in the end. I guess you could say not everything is as harmonious in Harmony, New Jersey, as it could be," she admitted with a shrug. "Let's just leave it at that."

"Well, don't get too carried away thinking about that," Gran-Gran said. "While you were out on your date with Gregg last night—"

"Date?" Tangie gasped. Did Gran-Gran really think that? "We were having dinner after auditions to discuss casting the play. That's all."

"Okay, well while you were having dinner with Gregg—for two and a half hours—Pastor Dave called, looking for you. He wants you to sing a solo at the Valentine's banquet next week. He said to pick out a love song and e-mail the title to him so Darla can find the piano music."

"W–what? But he's never even heard me sing. How does he

know that I can. . ." Tangie pursed her lips and stared at her grandmother.

"What?" Gran-Gran played innocent. "So, I told him you could sing. So what? And I happened to mention that you'd done that great Gershwin review a few years ago off-Broadway. What can I say? The man likes his Gershwin."

"Mm-hmm." Tangie sighed. "So, what am I singing?"

"Oh, that's up to you. Just something sweet and romantic. It is Valentine's, you know." Gran-Gran disappeared into the kitchen, chattering all the way about her favorite tunes from the forties and fifties.

Oh, Gran-Gran, you're the queen of setting people up, aren't you? You planned this whole thing.

Tangie sighed as she thought about Valentine's Day. Last year Tony had taken her to La Mirata, one of her favorite Italian restaurants in the heart of the city. It had been a magical night. This year would be a far cry from that romantic evening.

Not that romance with Tony was ever genuine. No, ever the actor, he'd managed to convince her she was his leading lady. But, in reality. . .

Well, to say there were others waiting in the wings would be an understatement.

Tangie put the cookies and soda down and went to the piano. Once there, she pulled back the lid, exposing the keys. She let her fingers run across them, surprised to hear the piano was in tune.

"We had it tuned the day you said you were coming," Gran-Gran hollered from the kitchen. "That way you wouldn't have any excuses."

Tangie shook her head and continued to play. Before long, she picked out the chords for one of her favorite Gershwin songs, "Someone to Watch over Me." After a couple times of running through it, she felt a bit more confident.

The words held her in their grip, as always. A good song

always did that—grabbed the listener and wouldn't let go. Just like a good book. Or a great play. Yes, anything artistic in nature had the capability of grabbing the onlooker by the throat and holding him or her captive for just a few moments.

Isn't that what the arts were all about? They lifted you from the everyday. . .the mundane. . .and took you to a place where you didn't have to think. Or worry. All you had to do was to let your imagination kick in, and the everyday woes simply faded away.

❧

Gregg fixed a peanut butter and jelly sandwich, carried it to the small breakfast table, and took a seat. He went back over every minute of today's meeting in his mind. Tangie had been awfully impressed with his brother, hadn't she? For some reason, a twinge of jealousy shot through Gregg as he thought about that.

Josh came across as a suave, debonair kind of guy, no doubt. But his motives weren't always pure, especially where women were concerned. And he seemed to have his eye on Tangie. Should Gregg say something to warn her?

No. Not yet, anyway. Right now, he just needed to finish up his sandwich and head over to Sweet Harmony. His mom needed him. And, unlike his brother, when Mom called. . . Gregg answered.

thirteen

As the evening of the Valentine's banquet approached, Tangie faced a mixture of emotions. She found herself torn between being drawn to Gregg and being frustrated with him. Clearly, they were as different as two people could possibly be. And while he seemed attracted to her—at least on the surface—Gregg had never actually voiced anything to confirm that. Other than that one impulsive kiss. The one he never mentioned, even in passing.

Maybe he had multiple personality disorder. Maybe the man who kissed her wasn't Gregg Burke. Maybe it was his romantic counterpart. Tangie laughed, thinking of what a funny stage play that would make. *Slow down, girl. Not everything is a story. Some things are very real.*

The fact that her heart was getting involved after only a few weeks scared Tangie a little. She didn't want to make the same mistake she'd made so many times before. . .falling for a guy just because they were working on a show together. She'd had enough of that, thank you very much. Still, Gregg was different in every conceivable way from the other men she'd known. And his heart for the Lord was evident in everything he did.

Tangie smiled, thinking about the night they'd posted the cast list. The children—well, most of them, anyway—had been ecstatic. Margaret had sulked, naturally, but even she seemed content by the time Tangie explained her role as narrator. Excited, even. Of course, they hadn't faced her mother yet. And then there was the issue of Josh. He'd shown more than a little interest in her, something which ruffled her feathers. She'd finally put him in his place, but would he behave himself during the rehearsals? Had she made a mistake by putting him in such a pivotal role?

With the casting of the show behind her, Tangie could focus on the Valentine's banquet. On the evening of the event, she looked through her clothing items for something appropriate to wear. Thanks to her many theater parties in New York City, she had plenty of eveningwear. She settled on a beautiful red and black dress with a bit of an Asian influence. Tony—her one-time Mr. Right—had said she looked like a million bucks in it. But then, he was prone to flattery, wasn't he?

At a quarter till seven, a knock sounded at the door.

"Come in." Tangie sat at the small vanity table, finishing up her makeup but paused to look up as Gran-Gran whistled.

"Tangie." Her grandmother's eyes filled with tears. "I don't believe it."

"Believe what?" She slipped her earrings on and gave herself one last glance.

Gran-Gran drew close. "You look so much like your mother did at this age. And I just had the strangest flashback."

"Oh?" Tangie looked at her with a smile. "What was it?"

Her grandmother's eyes filled with tears. "This was her bedroom, you know. And I remember the day she got married, watching her put on her makeup and fix her hair in that very spot." She pointed to the vanity table, then dabbed at her eyes. "Look at me. I'm a silly old woman."

Tangie rose from her seat and moved in her grandmother's direction. "There's nothing silly about what you just said. I think it's sweet. And it's fun to think that Mom used to get ready in this same room. I guess I never thought about it before." She pointed at her dress. "What do you think? Do I look okay?"

"Oh, honey." Gran-Gran brushed a loose hair from Tangie's face, "I've never seen you look prettier. In fact, I want to get some pictures of you to send to your parents. They're never going to believe you're so dolled up."

"Sure they will. Remember the bridesmaid's dress I wore at Taffie's wedding on the beach? And don't you remember those dresses we wore at Candy's wedding last year?"

"Yes." Gran-Gran nodded. "But I think tonight surpasses them all."

Gramps stuck his head in the door and whistled. "I'm gonna have the prettiest two women at the banquet. How lucky can one guy be?" After a chuckle, he headed off to start the car, hollering, "Don't take too long, ladies. The roads are bad and we'll need a little extra time."

Tangie donned her heavy winter coat and reached for a scarf. After one last glance in the mirror, she grabbed her purse and followed along on her grandmother's heels to the garage, where Gramps was waiting in the now-heated Ford.

"Are you ready for the program tonight?" Gran-Gran asked as they settled into the car.

"I guess so. I found the perfect song."

"Oh?"

"Gershwin, of course. 'Someone to Watch over Me.'"

"I heard you playing it. Of course, I've heard you play a great many things over the past few days. It's good to have music in the house again. But I'm tickled you chose that particular song. It's one of my favorites from when I was a girl."

"Really?"

"Oh yes. I used to be quite the performer. I'd stand in front of that vanity—the same one you used to put on your makeup—and hold a hairbrush in my hand, pretending it was a microphone. Then I'd sing at the top of my lungs. And I was always putting on little shows and such in the neighborhood."

"Yes, she's always been quite the performer," Gramps added. "She even had a starring role in a community theater show about twenty years ago. Back when we had a community theater, I mean. It's long since been torn down."

"So, what happened?" Tangie asked. "Why did you stop?"

Gran-Gran sighed. "I don't know. Just fizzled out, I guess."

"I can understand that."

"Dreams are like flowers, honey," her grandmother said. "They need watering and tending to. If you neglect them, well, they just die off."

Sad. But true. And hadn't Penny pretty much said the same thing? Dreams needed to be chased after. Tangie wondered if the Lord might be nudging her back to New York to pursue some of those dreams she'd given up on. Perhaps the answer would be clearer in time.

In the meantime, Tangie focused on her grandmother's words as they made the short drive to the church. When they arrived, Tangie searched for Darla, the pianist. Hopefully she would have time to run over her song one last time.

As she rounded the corner near the choir room, Tangie paused. The most beautiful tenor voice rang out. The voice drew her, much like one of the Pied Piper's tunes that captivated children.

She peeked inside the room and caught a glimpse of Gregg, dressed in a dark suit. He stood with his back to her, singing another one of her favorite Gershwin songs, "But Not for Me." She listened intently as he sang the bittersweet words about a man who feared he would never find love. Tangie heard genuine sadness in Gregg's voice. Either that, or his acting skills really were better than he'd let on.

She slipped into the room and sat in a chair at the back. When he finished, she applauded and he turned her way, his cheeks flashing red. "Tangie. I didn't know you were here."

She slowly rose and walked to the piano. "Dave asked me to sing tonight, too. Hope that's okay."

"Of course. He told me. Your grandmother thinks very highly of your singing abilities."

"Hmm." Tangie shrugged. "Well, we'll see if anyone else agrees, or if her opinion of me is highly overrated."

She handed her music to Darla, and the introduction for

"Someone to Watch over Me" began. With Gregg standing at her side, Tangie started to sing.

❧

Gregg could hardly believe what he was hearing. Tangie's singing voice blew him away. And as she sang the familiar words, he almost felt they were directed at him. *She's looking for someone to watch over her.*

Just as quickly, he chided himself. They were here to work together. Nothing more. Still, as the music flowed from page to page, Gregg found himself captivated by this chameleon who stood before him. She was both actress and singer. And amazing at both, from what he could tell. Not to mention beautiful. In this red and black number, she looked like something straight off the stages of Broadway.

When she ended the song, Gregg shook his head, but didn't speak. He couldn't, really. Not yet, anyway.

Thankfully, he didn't have to. Darla clapped her hands together and turned to him. "I have the most amazing idea," she said, turning pages in the Gershwin book. She dog-eared a couple of pages, then kept flipping, clearly not content as of yet with her choices. "You two need to sing a song together."

"W–what?" Tangie shook her head. "But the banquet starts in ten minutes and we haven't rehearsed anything."

"You won't need to." Darla began to play, her fingers practically dancing across the keys. "You two can pull off a last minute performance, no problem. Trust me. You don't need rehearsal time. You each have the most beautiful voices. And I'm sure the blend will be amazing." She turned to face Tangie. "Now, you sing alto, Tangie. And, Gregg, you sing lead."

"B–but. . ." He gave up on the argument after just one word because the first verse kicked in. He began to warble out the first words to "Embraceable You," fully aware of the fact that he was singing directly to—and with—one of the most beautiful women he'd ever laid eyes on. Within seconds, Tangie added a perfect harmony to his now-solid melody line and they were off and running. *Lord, what are You doing here? First I kiss her, now I'm singing her a love song?*

After just one verse, Darla stopped playing and looked back and forth between them, shaking her head. Her gaze landed on Tangie. "You know, for an actress, you're not giving this much effort."

"E–excuse me?" Tangie's eyes widened.

"You're not very believable, I mean. This is a love song. You two act like you're terrified of each other. Can't you hold hands and look each other in the eye while you sing? Something like that? Isn't that what they teach you to do on Broadway? To play the part?"

"Well, yes, but. . ."

Drawing in a deep breath, Gregg took hold of her hands. "We don't want to get Darla mad, trust me. I did that once in a vocal team practice and she knuckled me in the upper arm."

"Did not," Darla muttered.

"Did, too," he countered. Gregg turned to look at Tangie, unable to hide the smile that wanted to betray his heart. "We might as well go along with this. Besides, tonight is all about romance, and half the people in the room are huge Gershwin fans. So, why not?"

"O–okay."

Darla began the piece again, and this time Gregg held tight to Tangie's hands, singing like a man in love from start to finish. Tangie responded with passion in her eyes—and her voice. If he didn't know her acting skills were so good, Gregg would have to think she really meant the words of the song.

He could barely breathe as the music continued. The voice flowing out of her tonight was pure velvet. And the way they harmonized. . .he could hardly believe it. While he'd sung with hundreds of people over the years, none had blended with his voice like this. Never.

As they wrapped up the last line, Dave stuck his head in the door. "Gregg, are you ready?" He took one look at the two of them holding hands and stared in silence. "Whoa."

Tangie pulled her hands loose and started fidgeting with her hair. She reached to grab her purse and scooted past him. "I'll see you in the fellowship hall. Just holler when you're ready for me."

Darla rose from the piano bench and gave him a knowing look. She, too, left the room. Dave took a couple of steps inside. "Someone having a change of heart?"

"I. . ." Gregg shook his head. "I don't have a clue what's happening."

"That's half the fun of falling in love," Dave said, slapping him on the back. "What fun would it be if you knew what was coming? Let it be a surprise. Besides, you could use a few surprises in your life. You're a little. . .predictable."

"Not always," Gregg countered.

"Oh yeah?" Dave laughed. "Do you realize you always order the same meal at the diner?"

"Well, yeah, but. . ."

"And what about your clothes? Did you realize you always wear a blue button-up shirt on Fridays?"

"Well, that's because Friday was our school color day when I was a kid."

"This isn't grade school, my friend." Dave chuckled. "And what's up with your hair? You've combed it exactly the same way ever since I met you."

"I have?"

"You have. And I'd be willing to bet you're still listening to that same CD I gave you for Christmas last year."

"Well, it's a great CD. I love those songs."

"Mm-hmm." Dave paused, his eyes narrowing. "You eat the same foods, you keep the same routine, you wear the same clothes. And your office is meticulous. Can't you mess it up, even just a little? Do something different for a change! Live on the edge, bro."

Gregg sighed. "Okay, okay. . .so I'm predictable. But I'm

working on it. Wait till you see that new song we're doing in choir on Sunday. I'm trying to stretch myself."

Dave grinned. "That's great. But don't jump *too* far out of the box. Might scare people."

"There's little chance of that." Gregg chuckled as he thought about it. No, where music was concerned, he was liable to stick with what he knew. But in matters of the heart? Well, that was something altogether different.

❧

Tangie somehow made her way through the meal portion of the banquet, nervous about the music, which was scheduled to begin during dessert. Something rather magical had happened in that choir room, something undeniable. She and Gregg sang together as if they'd been born to do so, but there was more to it than that. Chemistry. That was really the only word to describe it. And not the kind in a science lab.

As she nibbled on her baked potato, Tangie caught a glimpse of Gregg, who was seated across the table and down a few feet. In his dark suit and tie, he looked really good. She watched as a couple of the young women from the church vied for his attention. Though polite, he didn't seem particularly interested in any of them.

"Where's Ashley tonight?" Tangie asked, turning to her grandmother.

"Ah. She's out with an old beau." Gran-Gran's eyebrows elevated. "A guy from college."

"Oh, I'm sorry she's not going to be here. I was looking forward to hanging out with her."

"Well, get to know some of the other people your age," her grandmother suggested. She nodded in Gregg's direction. "I see someone about your same age sitting right there."

"Gran-Gran. No matchmaking."

"Matchmaking? Me?" Her grandmother shook her head. "Heavens, no. I wouldn't think of it."

"Sure you wouldn't. And I'm pretty sure you didn't put

Darla up to any tricks, either."

"Darla? Hmm? What did you say, honey? I'm having a little trouble hearing you tonight with all of the people talking."

"Sure you are."

The meal wrapped up in short order, and the lights in the room went down as the small stage area at the front was lit. Tangie smiled at the decorations. Cupids, hearts, and candles. . . as far as the eye could see.

As Gregg sang his song, Tangie closed her eyes and listened. With her eyes shut, she could almost picture him singing on a huge stage at one of the bigger theaters in New York. He had that kind of voice—the kind that landed lead roles. Why hadn't he gone that direction? He could've made a lot of money with a voice like that.

Just as quickly, she knew the answer. His love was the Lord. . .and the church. She saw it on Sunday mornings as he led worship. She'd witnessed it on Thursday nights as she walked past the choir room and heard him leading the choir.

Still, as he crooned the familiar love song, she couldn't help but think of all the possibilities he'd missed out on.

When his song came to an end, Gregg introduced her to the dinner guests. "Ladies and gentlemen, one of our newest members—straight from the stages of New York City—Tangie Carini."

Gran-Gran nudged her. "Your turn, sweetie. Show 'em what you've got."

"I–I'll do my best," she whispered. "But remember, I'm an actress, not really much of a vocalist."

"Humph. That's for us to decide."

As she made her way to the stage, Tangie whispered a prayer. She somehow made it through her song, but found herself facing Gregg, who'd taken a seat at the table nearest the stage. The words poured forth, and she allowed them to emanate with real emotion. How wonderful would it be, to have someone to watch over her? To love her and care for her?

Someone with sticking power.

As the song came to a conclusion, the audience erupted in applause. Tangie's cheeks felt warm as she gave a little bow. Then, with her nerves climbing the charts, she nodded in Gregg's direction and he joined her on stage.

"We've decided to try our hand at a duet," he said, after taking the microphone in hand. "Though we haven't had a lot of practice." He turned to Tangie and whispered, "You ready for this?"

She nodded, realizing she was, indeed, ready. . .for anything life might throw her way.

fourteen

The Valentine's banquet ended on a high note, pun intended. Everyone in the place gathered around Tangie and Gregg after they sang, gushing with glowing comments. She heard everything from, "You two are a match made in heaven," to "Best harmony in Harmony!"

Oh, but it *had* felt good to sing with him, hadn't it? And gazing into his eyes, their hands tightly clasped, she could almost picture the two of them doing that. . .forever.

Of course, she might be leaving in April. That would certainly put a damper on forever. Still, she could imagine it all, if even for a moment.

After the crowd dissipated, Tangie helped her grandmother and some of the other women clean the fellowship hall. She noticed that Gregg disappeared and wondered about it, but didn't ask.

Gran-Gran's voice rang out, interrupting her thoughts. "Honey, they need your help in the choir room."

"They? Who are *they?*"

"Oh, I'm pretty sure Darla and Dave are in there with Gregg. Seems like someone said something about putting music away. Or maybe they said something about music for the Easter production. I can't remember." Gran-Gran yawned. "I just know I'm tired."

"Oh, I'm sure this can wait till later. I'm ready to go."

"No." With the wave of a hand, her grandmother shooed her out of the room. "You go on, now. Do whatever you have to do."

Tangie headed off to the choir room, where she found Gregg alone, seated at the piano. With his back turned to her, he didn't see—or hear—her enter. She found herself intrigued by the piece of music pouring out of him. It was truly one of the most beautiful melodies she'd ever heard. Truly anointed.

He continued to play and she drew near, pulling up a chair next to him. Not that he noticed. No, as the music poured forth, his eyes remained closed. For a moment, Tangie wondered if she might be invading his privacy. *Lord, is this how he worships?*

There wasn't time for a response. The music stopped abruptly and Gregg turned her way, a startled look on his face.

"I—I'm sorry." She stood. "I didn't mean to interrupt."

"No, it's fine." His eyes flashed with embarrassment. "I just needed a little alone time after that banquet. Might sound weird, but I usually don't leave the church until I've spent a little time on the piano. It helps me wind down."

"Makes perfect sense to me." After pausing a moment, she asked the question on her heart. "Did you write that piece?"

He nodded. "I have quite a few worship melodies like that. If you listen on Sunday mornings, sometimes I play them during the quiet times in worship, when people are at the altar praying. There's something about worship music that's so. . ."

"Anointed." They spoke the word together.

"Yes." Gregg nodded. "And to be honest, I like to close out the day with worship because it helps me put things in perspective."

"Me, too," she said. "But I usually just listen to CDs or songs on my MP3 player. Can you play something else?"

He looked her way, their eyes meeting for one magical moment. Then, just as quickly, he turned his attention to the keys. The music that poured forth was truly angelic. She'd never heard anything quite like it. Tangie closed her eyes, lifting her thoughts to the Lord.

As the song ended, she sighed. "Thank you for that. It's good to just slow down and spend some time focusing on the

Lord, especially after such a hectic day."

"It was hectic, wasn't it?"

"Yes." She smiled. "But it was wonderful, too. I had such a great time."

He gazed into her eyes, a hint of a smile gracing his lips. "I don't mind saying, you've got one of the best voices I've ever heard."

"I was just going to say the same thing to you." A nervous laugh erupted. Then Tangie glanced up at the clock on the wall and gasped. "Oh no. Gran-Gran and Gramps are waiting for me. I have to go."

"Kind of like Cinderella at the ball?"

She looked at Gregg, curious. "What do you mean?"

He shrugged. "Just when things were getting exciting, Cinderella took off. . .left the prince standing there, holding a shoe in his hand."

"Well, my feet are aching in these shoes, but I promise not to leave them with you." Tangie rose and grinned. *Though you definitely look like prince material in that suit.* "But I do have to go. Thanks again for the great evening."

"Hang on and I'll walk with you. I just need to turn out the lights in here." He led the way to the light switch by the door. As he flipped it, the room went dark. Standing there, so close she could almost feel his breath against her cheek, Tangie's heart began to race. Seconds later, she felt Gregg's fingertip tracing her cheekbone.

"Life is full of surprises, isn't it?" he whispered.

"Mm-hmm." She reached up with her hand to take his, then gave it a gentle squeeze.

He responded by drawing her into his arms and holding her. Just holding her. No kiss. No drama. Just a warm, embraceable moment, like they'd sung about.

Gregg finally released his hold and stepped back. "They're going to come looking for us if we don't get out there."

"R-right." Tangie smiled at him, wishing the moment

could have lasted longer. Still, she didn't want to keep her grandparents waiting.

She walked back into the fellowship hall, stunned to see Gran-Gran missing. "That's so weird. Well, I know Gramps was tired. They're probably waiting in the car." Gregg helped her with her coat, and she wrapped her scarf around her neck.

"I'll walk you out." Gregg turned out the lights and locked the door and they headed to the parking lot, chatting all the way.

She wanted to reach for his hand. In fact, she felt so comfortable around him that she almost did it without thinking. But Tangie stopped herself, realizing that others might see. She didn't want to get the rumor mill started.

When they reached the parking lot, she gasped. "What in the world?"

"Did they leave?" Gregg looked around.

"Surely not. Maybe they just took a spin around the block to warm up the engine or something like that."

She picked up her cell phone and punched in Gran-Gran's number. When her grandmother's sleepy voice came on the line, Tangie realized she must be in bed.

"Gran-Gran?"

"What, honey?"

"Did you forget something?"

"I don't think so." She gave an exaggerated yawn. "What do you mean?"

Tangie shivered against the cold, and Gregg pulled off his coat and draped it over her shoulders. She turned to him with a comforting nod as she responded to her grandmother. "I mean, you left me here."

"Oh, that." A slight giggle from the other end clued her in immediately.

"Gran-Gran, what are you up to?"

"Up to? We were just tired, honey. We're not spring chickens, you know. Gramps has to be home to take his blood pressure medication at a certain time every night."

"He took it before we left. I saw him with my own eyes. And besides, I was only in the choir room fifteen minutes," Tangie argued. "I thought you were waiting on me."

"We started to, but then I noticed Gregg's car was still there, and he lives so close and all. . ."

"Gran-Gran." Tangie shook her head. "You're up to tricks again."

"Me? Tricks?" Another yawn. "What do you mean?"

"Nothing. Just leave your granddaughter stranded in the cold on a winter's night. No problem."

Gran-Gran laughed aloud. "I daresay that handsome choir director will bring you home. And I'm sure there's a heater in his car. So, don't you worry, honey. Just enjoy your time together."

Enjoy our time together? Yep, we've been set up, all right.

As Tangie ended the call, she turned to Gregg, trying to decide how to tell him. Thankfully, she didn't have to.

"They left you?" he asked, his brow wrinkled in concern.

"Yep." She turned to face him with a sigh. "I don't believe it, but. . .they ditched me."

❧

Gregg couldn't help but laugh at the look on Tangie's face. "So, we've been set up."

"Looks that way."

"Someone's doing a little matchmaking."

"Gran-Gran, of course. But I didn't think she'd go this far."

Gregg reached to take Tangie's hand. "Oh, I'm not complaining, trust me. This is probably the first time in my life I'm actually thrilled to be set up."

"R—really?" Tangie's teeth chattered and he laughed.

"Let's get you out of the cold." He walked over to his car and opened the passenger side door. She scooted into the seat and smiled at him as he closed the door in the most gentlemanly fashion he could muster. Then, he came around to the driver's side and settled into his own seat. Turning the key in the ignition, a blast of cold air shot from the vents. "Sorry about that. Takes awhile for the air to warm up."

"Good things are worth waiting for," Tangie said, giving another shiver.

He looked her way and smiled. "Yes, they are."

Their eyes met for another one of those magical moments, one that set a hundred butterflies loose in his stomach.

Gregg finally managed to get a few words out. "I. . .I guess I'd better get you home."

They made the drive to Tangie's grandparents' house and Gregg pulled the car into the driveway, his nerves a jumbled mess.

Tangie smiled at him as he put the car into PARK. "Thanks for the ride. Sorry about all of this."

"Oh, I'm not, trust me." Gregg watched as she opened her door, but then stopped her before she stepped out. "Hey, can you wait just a minute?"

"Oh, sure." She looked at him with that piercing gaze, the one that made him a bumbling schoolboy once again. She pulled the door shut, then turned back to him. "What's up?"

"I, um. . .I just wanted to say something about the other night when I, um. . ."

"Ah." She smiled, suddenly looking like a shy kid. "*That.*"

"Yeah, that." He looked down to hide the smile that threatened to betray his heart. "First, I was out of line."

"Oh?" She sounded a little disappointed.

"Yes. I feel like I took advantage of the situation. But"—he looked at her—"I'm not sorry I did it."

In that moment, the tension in the car lifted. Tangie's voice had a childlike quality to it as she whispered, "I'm not sorry, either."

At once, Gregg felt as if his heart might burst into song. Maybe even another Gershwin tune. She wasn't sorry he'd kissed her. That answered every question.

"I'm usually the most predictable guy on planet Earth," he said. "But that kiss. . ."

She grinned. "Was unpredictable?"

"To say the least." He paused a moment. "It was downright impulsive. And it totally threw me." He couldn't stop the smile from creeping up. "In a good way, I mean."

"It feels good to be unpredictable every now and again, doesn't it?" She giggled, and he thought he might very well go sailing off into space.

Yes, if felt good. Mighty good. In fact, he could go on feeling this good for the rest of his life. "I want to say one more thing. I had a great time singing with you tonight. I felt like our harmony was. . ."

"Amazing?"

"Yes." He smiled. "Sometimes life does surprise you, doesn't it? And how interesting that two very different people could sound so totally perfect together."

"Mm-hmm." Tangie sighed. "Just goes to show you. . . We have to give things a chance."

"Yes, we do." He smiled, thankful she'd given him the prompt for what he wanted to say. "And that's really what I wanted to ask you. . .if you'd be willing. . .to give a boring, predictable guy like me a chance."

"You mean *un*boring and *un*predictable, right?" Tangie grinned, her eyebrows elevating mischievously. "I think you've crossed the line into a new life, my friend."

"You—you do?" Gregg never really had time to add anything more than that. Tangie's lips got in the way.

fifteen

Rehearsals for the children's production began the last Saturday in February. The children gathered in the sanctuary and, after a quick prayer, were immediately divided into two groups—singing and non-singing. Gregg took the vocalists into the choir room to practice, and Tangie worked with the actors and actresses. For weeks, she'd planned how the rehearsals would go, had even mapped them out on paper, accounting for every minute of time. But now that the moment had arrived, things didn't go exactly as planned.

For one thing, several kids were missing.

"Where's Margaret Sanderson?" she asked, looking around.

"Margaret's not going to be in the play," a little girl named Abigail said. "She's really mad."

"Oh?" Tangie forced herself not to knee-jerk in front of the kids, though everything inside her threatened to do so.

"She wanted to get the main part." Abigail shrugged. "But she didn't."

"All parts are equal in this play," Tangie explained to the group. "There's a saying in theater: 'There are no small parts, only small actors.' In other words, whether your part is little or big isn't the point. It's how much effort you put into it that counts."

"Well, she's not going to put any effort into it, 'cause she's not coming," Abigail said.

Tangie's mind reeled. She'd specifically asked Margaret if she would be willing to accept any role she received and the little girl had agreed. And now this? *We're not off to a very good start, Lord.*

Out of the corner of her eye, she caught a glimpse of Gregg's brother, Josh, as he swaggered up the center aisle of the church. Tangie glanced at the clock. Yep, just as she thought. He was ten minutes late. Looked like he wasn't taking his role very seriously, at least not yet.

He drew near and whispered, "Sorry I'm late," in her ear, then muttered something about his mom not feeling well. Tangie softened immediately. "Ah. Okay."

After a few seconds of glancing over her notes, she began to call the children to the stage. "Missy, you stand over here. Kevin, stand over there. Cody, take your place upstage right."

"Upstage right?" He gave her a funny look, and she pointed to the spot where he needed to go.

Once all of the players were in place, Tangie clapped her hands. "Now, let's do a quick read-through of the first scene. Starting with the narrator."

She looked center stage, remembering Margaret—the narrator—was missing. "Hmm. I guess I'll read the narrator's lines." She began to read, but off in the corner one of the boys distracted her. Tangie stopped and looked at Cody, who'd just punched Kevin in the arm. "Cody! What are you doing?"

"He called me a chicken."

"Well, you *are* a chicken," Kevin said with a shrug. "Aren't you playing the part of a chicken in the play?"

"Yeah, but that doesn't mean I want to." Cody groaned, his hands still knotted into tight fists. "My mom is making me do this dumb play just like she made me do the last one. I'm going to be a lousy chicken."

Kevin began to squawk like a chicken and before long, everyone was laughing.

"Hey, at least you're not one of the singing rabbits like me," one of the other boys said. "Can you imagine telling your friends at school you have to wear rabbit ears in a play?"

"Yeah? Well what about me? I'm a sheep," one of the little girls said with a sour look on her face. Everyone began to *baa* and before long, the stage was filled with squawking, bleating, squealing noises representing the entire animal kingdom.

Finally, Tangie had had enough. She felt like throwing her hands up in the air and walking away. If she felt this way on the first day, what was the week of performance going to be like?

A shiver ran down her spine as she thought about it. *One mountain at a time, Tangie. One mountain at a time.*

≈

Gregg sat at the piano, playing a warm-up for the children in the choir. As they "la-la-la'd," he listened closely. They sounded pretty good, for a first rehearsal. One or two of the kiddos were a little off-pitch, but this was certainly better than the Christmas production. Tangie was right—it worked out best for the non-singers to take acting roles. That way, everyone was happy. Well, mostly. Some of the boys still balked at the various roles they'd been given, but they'd get over it. In time. With therapy. Perhaps before they went off to college.

Out of the corner of his eye, Gregg saw someone come in the back of the room. Margaret Sanderson. According to his schedule, Margaret wasn't supposed to come to the vocal room for another half hour. Perhaps she'd missed the memo. He paused as she approached the piano.

"My mom said I should talk to you." She pushed a loose blond hair behind her ear.

"Oh?"

Margaret crossed her arms at her chest and glared at him. "She's mad."

"Ah ha."

"Really mad." Margaret began to tap her foot on the floor.

"Margaret, I'm sorry she feels that way." Gregg lowered his voice. "But this isn't the time to talk about it. Perhaps you could tell your mom that I'll be happy to meet with her after we're done with the rehearsal."

Margaret sighed. "I don't think she'll come." She shuffled off to the side of the room and took a seat, a scowl on her face.

Wow. Tangie was right about that one. The child did have some major attitude problems. Even more so when she didn't get her way.

The rehearsal continued with few mishaps. Afterward, Margaret's mother met with Gregg in the hallway, voicing her complaints, one after the other.

Gregg did his best to stay cool. "Mrs. Sanderson, I'm sure you can see that we have a lot of talented children in this congregation."

"Humph."

"And we did our best to put the children in the roles where they could grow and develop."

"How is playing the narrator going to help Margaret develop? There's no vocal solo. We're talking about a child with an extraordinary gift here, one who's going to go far. . .if she's given the right opportunities."

"Actually, she does have a solo in the midst of the group numbers. And the narrator threads the show together, after all. Margaret is onstage more than any other character, in fact. So, in that sense, I guess you could say that she's got the lead role."

Mrs. Sanderson's face tightened even further—if that were possible. "Mr. Burke, you and I both know that Margaret should have been given the role of the littlest lamb, the one with the beautiful solo. Instead, you gave it to an unknown."

An unknown? Was she serious? These were children.

For a moment, Gregg had the funniest feeling he'd slipped off into another galaxy, one where determined stage mothers ruled the day and lowly music directors became their subjects. Only, he didn't want to subject himself to this madness—not now, not ever. He immediately prayed that the Lord would guard his tongue.

"Mrs. Sanderson, I'm sorry you and Margaret are disappointed, and I will understand if you withdraw her from the play. However, I want you to know that we've prayed over these decisions. At length. And we feel sure we've placed the children into the roles they have for a reason."

The woman's countenance changed immediately. "So, this is God's doing? Highly unlikely. The God I serve doesn't like to see church folks embarrassed. And this play is going to be an embarrassment to our congregation, just like the last one."

Hang on a minute while I pull the knife from my heart, and then I'll respond. Gregg exhaled slowly. *One. Two. Three. Four. Five.* Then he turned to her, determined to maintain his cool.

"I'm not saying we're perfect, and I certainly can't guarantee this show will be any better than the last one. I can only assure you that we prayed and placed the children accordingly. Again, if you want to pull Margaret from the play, we will miss her. But we will certainly understand."

At this point, he caught a glimpse of Tangie coming up the hallway. She looked as exhausted as he felt. Mrs. Sanderson turned to her, an accusing look in her eye. "We all know who's to blame for this, anyway."

"W–what?" Tangie looked back and forth between them, a shocked look on her face. "What am I being blamed for?"

"You know very well. You waltz in here in those crazy clothes and with that ridiculous spiked-up hair and stir up all kinds of trouble. Obviously, you need glasses."

"G–glasses?"

"Yes. Otherwise you would have already seen that Margaret is the most talented child in this church." Mrs. Sanderson grabbed a teary Margaret by the hand and pulled her down the hallway, muttering all the way.

Tangie looked at Gregg, her eyes wide. "Do I even want to know what that was about?"

"No." He gestured for her to follow him into the choir room, where they both dropped into chairs. "Let's just say she was out of line and leave it at that. And I also need to say that you were right all along about Margaret. Though, to be fair,

I can't really blame the child when it's a learned behavior."

"Right." Tangie nodded. "I've met so many drama divas through the years. . .they're getting easier to recognize. Still, I can't help but think Margaret is supposed to be in this play. The Lord wants to soften her heart."

"Sounds like He needs to start with her mom."

Tangie gave Gregg a look of pure sweetness and reached out to touch his arm. "Let's pray about that part, too, okay? I honestly think God has several plans we're unaware of here. Putting on a show is always about so much more than just putting on a show. You know? God is always at work behind the scenes, doing things we can't see or understand. We see the outside. He sees the inside."

Gregg took her hands in his and sighed. "Tangie, you've managed to sum up so many things in that one statement."

"What do you mean?" She looked puzzled.

"I mean, man looks at the outward appearance. God looks at the heart. He's not interested in the clothes we wear— colorful, outlandish, or otherwise."

"Hey, now."

Gregg chuckled. "You get what I'm saying. He's too busy looking at our hearts. And you're right. He's working behind the scenes. I know He has been in my life. . .ever since you arrived. And now you've made me look for the deeper meaning, not just in a kids' play, but in my own life. That's one of the things I love most about you. You *always* look for deeper meaning in everything."

Almost immediately, he realized what he'd said: *One of the things I love most about you.* Wow. A slip of the tongue, perhaps, or was Gregg really starting to fall in love? Gazing into Tangie's eyes, he couldn't help but think it was the latter.

sixteen

On the Monday after the first rehearsal, Tangie went to work at the bakery. The place was buzzing with customers from early morning till around eleven. Then things began to slow down.

"People like their sweets early in the morning," Tangie observed, pulling an empty bear claw tray from the glass case.

"And late in the afternoon. The after-school crowd can be quite a handful." Penny wiped her hands on her apron, then leaned against the counter and took a drink from a bottle of water.

"How are you feeling, Penny?"

Penny shrugged as she went to work putting icing on some éclairs. "Chemo's making me pretty squeamish. I've lost ten pounds in the last three weeks alone. And I want to pull this wig off and toss it across the room. Makes my head hot. And it itches."

Tangie offered up a woeful smile. Penny's last statement confirmed a suspicion she'd had all along. So, she did wear a wig. The hair seemed a little too perfect. But if anyone deserved to look extra-special, Penny did. Especially now.

Tangie paused to whisper a little prayer for her new friend. Penny had made it clear how she felt about the Lord, but that didn't stop Tangie. She'd started praying daily about how to reach out to her. What to say. What not to say. She didn't want to get in the way of what God might be doing in Penny's life. *Use me in whatever way You choose, but help me not to overstep my bounds.*

Though she'd worked several days at the bakery now, Tangie still felt a sense of disconnect between herself and

Penny. Seemed like the older woman kept her at arm's length. Not that Tangie blamed her. Penny had plenty of other things on her mind right now.

In the meantime, Tangie had a couple of questions, from one female to another. "Penny, can I ask you something?"

"Sure, kid." She continued icing the éclairs, never looking up. Still, Tangie knew she was paying attention.

"Have you ever been in love?"

Penny snorted, nearly dropping her icing bag. "Only ten or twenty times."

"Really?" Tangie looked at her, stunned. "Are you serious?"

"Yes." Penny nodded, then went right back to work. "Remember, I told you those church folks didn't know what to make of me. I was a single mom with two boys and no husband in sight. I guess I was so desperate to find a father for them that I checked under every bush."

"Including the church."

Penny shrugged. "Maybe my motives for attending weren't exactly pure. But, hey, I thought a good Christian man would be just the ticket for my kids, ya know? Most of the ones I knew were pretty nice."

"But, you never found one?"

"Oh, I found a few." She winked. "Problem was, a couple were already involved with other women. And I, um. . .well, I broke up a couple of relationships."

"Ah." Tangie pondered those words. "But you never married any of the men you fell for?"

"No." Penny's expression changed. "Never found one that really suited me or my boys."

"How did Gregg end up working in a church, then?" Tangie began to stack fresh bear claws on the empty tray, more than a little curious about the answer to this question.

Penny closed the glass case and shrugged. "There was one man, a youth pastor, who took an interest in the boys when they were in their teens. Offered to drive them to church.

Even paid for Gregg to have voice lessons. He was a great guy. And I seem to recall a female choir teacher at school who spent a little extra time with him. She was a churchgoer. So, I guess he got sucked in that way."

"Ah." So not everyone had rejected them, then. After a moment's pause, Tangie couldn't hold back one particular question. "Has, um. . .has Gregg mentioned anything to you about the play we're doing with the kids?"

"Heavens, yes." Penny laughed as she began to roll out dough for cinnamon rolls. "I've heard all about it. He says you wrote it, too. Is that right?"

"Yeah."

"He told me about the singing rabbits and the little sheep. That part sounded cute. And then there was something about a chicken hatching out of an egg. Did he get that part right?"

"He did." Tangie realized just how silly the whole thing sounded, when described in only a sentence or two. Still, the idea worked for the kids, even if the grown-ups couldn't quite figure it out.

"Well, all I know is, it's a kids' play and I'm no kid." Penny went off on a tangent, going on and on about singing rabbits and dancing chickens. Tangie couldn't tell if she was being made fun of, or if Penny really found the whole thing entertaining.

"I want you to make me a promise." Tangie stopped her work for a moment. She took Penny's hand and squeezed it. "Don't let anyone else's opinions sway you. Promise me you'll come see the play for yourself. The performance is in a couple of weeks. You decide if it's too much fluff or if it's something the kids can relate to."

"You're asking me to take sides?"

"No. I really want to know what you think. Besides, Gregg is working hard at this and I know he'd love it if you came."

Penny shook her head. "He knows me better than that. I haven't graced the doors of a church in years."

"Well, this Easter might just be a good time to give it a try. What have you got to lose, anyway?"

Penny snorted, then turned back to her work, muttering under her breath. Still, Tangie would not be swayed. Somehow, knowing that this woman—this wonderful, witty woman—was Gregg's mom, made her want to pray all the harder. . .not just for her healing, but for her very soul.

❧

On Monday afternoon, just as Gregg closed the door to his office, his cell phone rang. He looked down at the caller ID and smiled. "Hey, Mom," he answered. "What's up?"

"Pull out your rabbit ears, son. Mama's coming to church."

"W–what?" Maybe he was hearing things. "What did you say?"

"Said I'm coming to church. Oh, don't get all worked up. I'm not coming this Sunday or even next. But you give me the date for that rabbit and chicken show you and Tangie are directing and I'll be there for that."

"Mom, I really wish you'd come on a regular Sunday first. I think your opinion of me will be much higher."

"Are you saying the play's going to be awful?" she asked.

"Well, I can't imagine it will be awful," he said. "Not with Tangie behind the wheel. But let's just say we're off to an interesting start."

"Interesting is good." She let out a yelp, followed by, "Oops! Gotta go. Burned the oatmeal raisin cookies."

As she disappeared from the line, Gregg pondered his mother's words: *"Pull out your rabbit ears, son. Mama's coming to church."*

He couldn't help but laugh. After all these years, the Lord had finally figured out a way to get his mom back in church. And to think. . .she was coming because of a goofy play about singing rabbits. Gregg shook his head, and then laughed. In fact, he laughed so loud—and so long—that the door to Dave's office opened.

"Everything okay out here?" Dave gave him a curious look.

"Yes, sorry." Gregg chuckled. "It's just. . .the strangest thing has happened. I think God has cracked open my mom's shell." Images of the four-foot Easter egg floated through his mind, and Gregg laughed again.

"Oh?" Dave gave him a curious look.

"Let's just say God is using Tangie in more ways than we thought. She's somehow managed to convince my mom to come to church to see the play."

"Oh, really?" Dave's face lit into a smile and he whacked Gregg on the back. "Well, why didn't you say so? That's awesome news, man."

"Yes, awesome." Just as quickly, the laughter stopped.

"You okay?"

"Yeah." He nodded toward Dave's office. "Is it okay if I come in?"

"Of course. I'm done with my work for the day."

Gregg's emotions took a bit of a turn.

"Why don't you tell me what's going on?" Dave took a seat behind his desk.

"Ever since my mom was diagnosed, I've been so worried that she might. . ." He didn't say the word for fear it might somehow make it true.

"You're afraid she might not make it." Dave leaned his elbows on the desk and gazed at Gregg. "Is that it?"

"Yes. And I think Josh must be worried about that, too. That's why he came back to Harmony, I think. But neither of us has said it out loud. Till now."

"It's good to get it off your chest," Dave said. "Helps you see what you're really dealing with."

"I've been trying to figure out a way to witness to her for weeks now," Gregg admitted. "And every attempt has failed. I couldn't get that woman through the doors of a church if my life depended on it. And now Tangie's done it with a goofy kids' musical."

"First of all, you've been living your life in front of your mom. That's the best witness of all. Second, we can never predict what might—or might not—be a good avenue to get someone in church. That's why we try so many different things. Different things appeal to different people."

"Right." Gregg sighed.

Dave paused a moment, rolling a pen around the desk with his index finger. Finally he looked up. "Can I ask you a question?"

"Sure."

"You somehow feel responsible for what's happened to your mom?"

"Responsible? For her cancer?" Gregg tugged at his collar, unhappy with the turn this conversation had taken.

"Well, not just the cancer. I mean the way her life has turned out. The fact that she's in her early sixties and living alone."

"Ah." Gregg didn't answer for a minute. He needed time to think about what Dave had said. "I guess I do in some ways. I was always the man of the house, you know?"

"Right."

"Had to practically raise Josh. There was no dad around to do it. And I always took care of everything for my mom. I thought I could save the day. You know?"

"I know. I'm an oldest son, too."

"As a kid, I prayed every day for a dad. And when Mom married Steve—my brother's father—I thought I'd finally found one. But then. . .well, anyway, that didn't pan out. But I guess there's some truth to the idea that I somehow feel responsible for my mom. That's why this cancer thing has been so hard."

"You can't fix it."

"R–right." Gregg sucked in a breath, willing the lump in his throat to dissolve. "I, um, I want to see her healed. Whole. And in church, going to those crazy teas and socials and stuff with the other ladies. She's all alone over there at that shop and I feel so. . ."

"Responsible."

"Yeah. That's why I spend so much time with her and make sure I call her every day."

"Gregg, it's natural for the oldest son to feel responsible, especially one who had to be both father and son at the same time. But I want to free you up by telling you something. Only God can be God."

"W—what?"

"Only God can be God. You can't fill His shoes. They're too big. You've taken on the responsibility of looking after your mom, and that's a good thing. Especially during the chemo. But she's a feisty one. Independent."

"Always has been."

"Yes. And you can't change her now any more than you could when you were little, no matter how hard you try."

"I know." Gregg slumped down in his chair, thinking about Dave's words. "But that's never stopped me from trying."

"God has a plan, and it's bigger than anything you could concoct. He sees the whole stage of our lives. Knows whether we're going to move upstage or down. Knows if the next song is going to be a heart-wrenching melody or a song and dance number. So, go ahead and pray for her. Spend time with her. Make sure her needs are met. But don't overstep your bounds, and don't take on guilt that isn't yours. You were never intended to save your mother's soul."

"W—what?"

"You heard me. You can plant the seeds. You've already done it, in fact. You've lived your life in front of her, expressed your faith and not held anything back. She's been watching those things, I guarantee you. But, Gregg, it's not your fault she hasn't come to know the Lord yet."

At this point, the dam broke. In one sentence, Dave had freed him from the guilt he'd carried for years. He'd never admitted it to anyone but himself, of course, but that's exactly what he'd believed. . .that he had somehow been responsible, even for his mother's very soul.

Dave rose from his chair and came to Gregg's side of the desk. He laid his hand on his shoulder and spoke in a gentler voice than before. "Witnessing to someone isn't like writing one of your songs."

"What do you mean?"

"I mean, when you write a song, you control where the notes go. Whether the melody moves up or down. When you witness to someone, it's like throwing a few notes out into space and then handing the melody off to that person and to God. It's up to them how the song turns out. Not you."

Gregg thought about Dave's words as he left the office. In fact, he couldn't get them off of his mind for the rest of the evening. By the time he rolled into bed that night, he'd made up his mind to let the Lord write the song that was his mother's life.

seventeen

The following Saturday, rehearsals for the play moved forward. This time, things were even more chaotic than before. For one thing, Josh didn't show up. Tangie asked Gregg about him about five minutes after two, the projected start time.

"Have you heard from your brother?"

Gregg shook his head. "I know he's been staying at Mom's place, but I don't have a clue why he's not here."

"Ah. I'll try your mom's phone then." Tangie punched in the number, but there was no answer. She turned back to Gregg with a sigh. "Do you think we made a mistake casting him in such a large part? What if he doesn't show?"

"Hmm. I don't have a clue. But I'll try him on his cell." Gregg did just that, but Josh didn't answer. Looked like Tangie would have to read the lines of the Good Shepherd from off-stage. Not that it really mattered. Nothing today seemed to be going according to plan. A couple of the kids were missing, due to the stomach flu. And the ones who attended were rowdier than usual. Take Cody, for instance. Tangie hardly knew what to do with him. As the rehearsal blazed forward, he ran from one side of the stage to the other, making airplane noises, disrupting the work at hand.

Finally, Tangie snapped. "Cody, I'm trying to block this scene, but it's difficult with you moving all over the stage."

That stopped him in his tracks. He froze like a statue, then turned to her in slow motion, an inquisitive look on his face. "What does *block* mean?"

"To block a scene means I tell the players where to stand and where to move. When I say move downstage left, you go here." She pointed. "And when I say, "Move to center stage,

125

you go here." She pointed to the center of the stage and the kids responded with a few "Ah's" and "Oh's."

Oh, if only she could block the kids in real life. Tell them where and when to move. Then they would surely be more obedient. Unfortunately, the characters in her play were better behaved than the kids performing the parts. Over that, she had no control.

Control. Hmm. Seemed she'd lost it completely over the past couple of weeks. And with the Easter production just a month away, Tangie felt like throwing in the towel. But every time she reached that point, the Lord whispered a few words of encouragement in her ear, usually through someone like Gran-Gran or Gregg. Then determination would settle in once again. Tangie would stick with this, no matter what.

Thankfully, there was one piece of good news. A humbled Margaret had come to her during the second rehearsal, asking if she could still play the role of the narrator. Tangie wasn't sure what was behind Margaret's change of heart, but had smiled and responded with, "Of course, honey."

Looked like the Lord was up to something in the child's life. Could it be the result of Tangie's and Gregg's prayers, perhaps? Surely faith really did move mountains.

She watched from the edge of the stage as Margaret delivered each line with rehearsed perfection. Then Tangie turned to Annabelle, listening carefully as the youngster sang her first solo. The precious little girl, though shy, proved to be a great lead character, in spite of her inexperience.

About halfway into the final scene, Gregg's phone rang. "Sorry," he called out. He sprinted to the far side of the stage. From where she stood, Tangie could see him talking to someone, with a look of concern in his eyes. Glancing at her watch, she took note of the time. Three fifteen. The parents would be arriving soon, and she needed to update them on costume requirements. Still, she couldn't focus on that right now. No, she couldn't see past Gregg's wrinkled brow to think of anything else. Something had happened, but what?

When he ended the call, he took a few steps her way and whispered in her ear. "That was Josh. He's taken Mom to the hospital in Trenton. She's had a really bad reaction to her latest round of chemo."

"Oh, no."

Up on the stage, the kids began to recite lines on top of each other, most of them standing in the wrong places or facing the wrong way. Tangie would have to correct them later. Right now she needed to hear the rest of the story about Penny.

Gregg sighed. "She's been having trouble keeping anything down since her last treatment. She's a little dehydrated, is all. They've got her hooked up to IVs."

"Do you need to go? I can handle the kids."

"No, Josh said they're just keeping her on fluids another hour or so and then releasing her. He, um. . .he asked if I would read his lines for him." Gregg smiled. "Actually, he told me how much he missed being with the kids and how much he's looking forward to being in the show."

"Aw, I'm so glad. Maybe God is working on him."

"No doubt. He's also using this situation with Mom—and the play—to accomplish something pretty amazing."

"Sounds like it." Tangie turned her attention back to the kids, who were now scattered every which way across the stage. "Boys and girls, we need to run though that scene again," she called out. "I noticed that some of you weren't standing in the right places and a few of you need to work on your projection skills. Give it your best. Okay?"

They hollered out a resounding, "Okay!" and she began again. Still, as the rehearsal plowed forward, Tangie's thoughts were a hundred miles away.

With a heavy heart, she did her best to focus on the kids.

❧

After the children departed, Gregg and Tangie spent some

time cleaning up the mess the kids had left behind in the sanctuary. Then she headed to the office to use the copier. Gregg retreated to the choir room, taking a seat at the piano. Before touching his fingers to the keys, he made another quick call to Josh, and was grateful to hear his mom was now on her way home from the hospital.

Gregg's fingers pressed down on the ivory keys, and he felt instant relief. As the melody to one of his most recent compositions poured out of his fingertips, he reflected on the conversation he'd had with Dave about his mother less than a week ago. "Lord, I don't understand." He pounded out a few more notes. "Why don't you just reach down and touch her? Heal her? Why does she have to go through all of this?"

A few more notes rose and fell from the keys and then he stopped. Gregg stared at his trembling hands, realizing just how worked up he was. He shook his head, feeling anger rise to the surface like the foam on top of his coffee.

"What is it, Gregg?"

He turned as he heard Tangie's voice. She stood behind him, holding a stack of papers in her hand. When he shook his head again, she placed the papers on the top of the piano, then reached out and put her hands on his shoulders. He relaxed at her touch. Tangie offered a gentle massage as he returned to the keys once more. When he finally stopped playing, she whispered, "What has you so upset? The news about your mom, or something to do with the play?"

"Both." He played a few more notes, finally pausing again.

"I'm ready to listen whenever you want to talk."

This time, Gregg pulled his hands away from the keys. His thoughts shifted to the kids, then back to his mom.

"Might sound crazy," he said at last, "but when I see Cody, I see myself at that age." He turned to face Tangie, emotion welling inside of him.

"You were rowdy and unmanageable and sang in twelve keys at once?" The laugh lines around her eyes told him she didn't quite believe his story. "I'm sorry, but after getting to know you, I'd have to say that's a pretty tough sell. Not buying it."

"No. Just the opposite. But I was the kid from the single family home with the mother who never seemed to fit in." He paused a moment, then whispered, "Did you hear about his mom?"

"Brenna?" Tangie took a seat on the piano bench next to Gregg. "What about her?"

"You know about her wedding and all that."

"Right." Tangie smiled. "Your mom is doing the wedding cake."

Gregg sighed. "Not anymore. Cody took me aside after the rehearsal and told me the wedding is off. Phillip took off to Minnesota without so much as a word of warning to either of them. He sent Brenna an e-mail after he arrived."

"Oh, that poor woman." Tangie rested her head against Gregg's. "And Cody. I can't even imagine how he must feel."

"I can." He drew in a deep, calculated breath as the memories flooded over him. "I grew up in the same situation basically, but back then, people in churches weren't always as kind to single moms. I'm not sure you would believe me if I told you some of the stuff we went through."

"Surely that didn't happen here. . .in Harmony?"

"No, I grew up in a small town called Wallisville, not far from here. Just small enough for everyone to know everyone's business, if you know what I mean."

Tangie laughed. "Harmony feels like that to me, after living in Atlantic City, then the Big Apple."

"Well, I'm talking about a group of people who weren't as kind as the people from Harmony. Instead of befriending my mother, they judged her. They were pretty harsh, actually."

"Whoa." After pausing for a moment, she added, "I know what it feels like to be judged, trust me. Been through my share of that."

A pang of guilt shot through him, and for good reason.

Hadn't he once made assumptions about her, based on her appearance?

"Here's the thing. . ." He rested his palms against the edge of the piano bench and peered into her eyes. "My mom wasn't married when she had me."

"Right, I know. She told me all about that." Tangie nodded. "But that's not so uncommon these days, and it's certainly not the fault of the child."

"Oh, that's not what I was getting at. It's just that I was always looking for a father figure. Kind of like Cody." Gregg leaned back in his seat to finish the story. "My mom married Josh's dad when I was three. My dad never even stuck around to see me born. To my knowledge, he has no idea who I am or where I am."

"I—I'm sorry, Gregg."

He shrugged it off. "Anyway, when Mom married Steve, she was already pregnant with Josh. They had him a few months later, but the marriage ended before his first birthday, so it was a double slam-dunk. I *finally* had someone to play a fatherly role and he didn't stick around. That's why. . ." He groaned. "That's why I empathize so much with Cody. It has nothing to do with his ability to sing, or the lack thereof. It's just his situation."

"Well, let me ask you a question," Tangie said, the tenderness in her voice expressing her concern. "Your mom told me a little of this, but she mentioned a couple of specific people who took an interest in you."

"What do you mean?"

"I mean, you eventually got your life on the right track. And you figured out you could sing. Who were those people who took the time to pour into your life? Who led you to the Lord? Who stirred up your gifts?"

"Oh, that's easy. One of the men in our church always treated me kindly. Mr. Jackson. It was through his witness that I came to know Jesus as my Savior. And as for the music,

I have my sixth grade choir teacher, Mrs. Anderson, to credit with that. She went to our church, too." As he spoke her name, a rush of feelings swept over him. He hadn't thought about her in years. "To this day, I still remember the joy in her eyes as she talked to me about music and the tenderness in her voice as she responded to my never-ending questions."

Tangie looked at him with interest. "Okay. So, she saw a spark of something in you and fanned it into a flame."

"Right. I remember the day she asked my mother to come to one of those parent-teacher meetings. She told my mom that I was born to sing, that I'd been given a gift."

"Sounds like she and Mr. Jackson played a pretty big role in your life."

"Actually. . . ," Gregg felt tears well up in his eyes as he thought about it, "I used to credit them with saving my life. I was at a crossroads that year. I was going to go one way or the other. And they caught me just in time to point me down the right road. The right road for me, I mean."

"Wow. That's pretty amazing. God's timing is perfect."

"It is." *Thank You, Lord. How often I forget.*

"Okay, well let's go back to talking about Cody, then," Tangie said, her eyes now glowing. "We just need to figure out what his real gift is, so we can begin to stir it."

"Well, he's not a singer, that's for sure." Gregg groaned. "Not even close."

"He does have some minor acting ability."

"Acting up, you mean." Gregg grinned.

"Well, that, too. I could probably turn him into an actor if I could just keep him focused, but I haven't been able to do that," Tangie admitted. "Have you ever heard him talk about anything else?"

"I know he wanted to play baseball last year, but his mom couldn't afford to sign him up. I heard all about it."

"Really?" Tangie's eyes widened in surprise. "Well, I'm not a huge sports fan—haven't really had time to focus on any of them—but it might be fun to test the waters with Cody. When does the season start?"

"Oh. This coming week, I think. I saw a poster at the grocery store just last night."

"Well, here's an idea. If his mom can't afford to sign him up, why don't we raise the funds through the church's benevolence ministry and do it ourselves?"

"Baseball?" Gregg groaned. "I'm terrible at baseball. Don't even like to watch it. It's so. . .slow."

"I know. I feel the same way, but we're probably biased. Besides, I'm not asking you to *play* baseball, just to watch Cody do it. Help him discover his dream. If it is his dream, I mean." Tangie laughed. "It's so hard for me, as an artist, to understand the love of sports. But I suppose some people are as passionate about baseball and basketball as I am about acting and singing."

Gregg shook his head. "Crazy, right?"

"Very. But I definitely think this is something we can do. His mom is probably plenty distracted right now, and I know her finances are probably tapped out, like so many other single moms. We can do this for her. Don't you think?"

Gregg didn't have to think about it very long. "It's the perfect idea. We should do it. And when we do. . ." He looked at her with a smile. "He's going to need someone in the crowd, cheering him on. Want to come to a few practices with me?"

Tangie paused. "If. . .if I'm still here."

Gregg's heart hit the floor. "Are you still thinking of leaving?"

She released a sigh as she gazed at him with pain in her eyes. "I don't know, Gregg. If you'd asked me a couple weeks ago, I would've said yes in a heartbeat. I have so many opportunities waiting for me in New York. But now. . ." She shrugged. "Now I'm not sure which way to turn. But I promise to pray about it."

"Me, too." In his heart, Gregg wanted to add, "I'll pray that

God keeps you here, in Harmony." However, he knew better. Tangie needed to chase after her dreams, too.

Even if they didn't include him.

eighteen

The week before the Easter performance, the kids met with Tangie and Gregg for their first dress rehearsal. Although Gramps had worked long and hard on building the set pieces, he hadn't quite finished several of them. And though the kids had been told to have all of their costumes ready, many did not. Tangie ran around like a chicken with her head cut off—ironic, in light of the many chicken costumes—looking for feathers, rabbit ears, and so forth. She tried to keep her cool, but found it difficult.

In fact, she couldn't think of one thing that had gone as planned, and now that the performance date was approaching, Tangie had to wonder if she'd made a mistake in promising she could pull this off.

As she paused to pin a tiny microphone on a little girl, her thoughts gravitated to a call she'd received just this morning from Marti in New York, urging her to come back for auditions for *A Woman in Love*. Tangie's heart twisted within her as she contemplated the possibilities.

"Vincent says he's had his eye on you for two years," Marti had said. "He thought you did a great job in *Brigadoon* and wants to see you audition for the role of Gina in his new play. You're coming, right? This is the opportunity of a lifetime, Tangie. It's what you've waited for—the lead in a Broadway show."

"I don't know." Tangie's response had been hesitant, at best.

It sounded wonderful, of course, especially in light of the chaos she was facing with the kids. But every time she thought about leaving Gregg. . .well, the lump that rose in her throat grew harder and harder to swallow. She'd fallen for him, from his schoolboy haircut to his geeky tennis shoes. She loved him, and there was no denying it.

Of course, they hadn't really had time to develop their relationship. Who had time to date with a show underway? But if she stayed in Harmony after the production, there would be plenty of time to see where life—and love—might take them. Right?

Oh, Lord, show me what to do. I don't want to miss You this time. If this opportunity on Broadway is what You have for me, then speak clearly, Lord. But if I'm supposed to stay here. . .

The road back to New York might not be a long one, but from where she stood, it seemed like a million miles.

"Miss Tangie!" Cody's scream startled Tangie back to reality.

"W–what, honey?"

"I can't go out there wearing this costume." He pointed to his chicken suit, and a sour expression crossed his face.

Tangie tried to hide her smile as she responded. "Why not?"

"My friends will make fun of me." He plopped down on his bottom on the stage. "Besides, I think I'm getting sick. I have the flu." He sneezed, but she could tell it was forced.

"Well, I'll tell you what," she said, "if you will do this one show dressed as a chicken, I promise never to cast you in a part like this again."

"I don't want to be in any show again," he muttered, pulling at his feathers. "When will people get that?"

Oh, she got it all right. And she had a wonderful surprise for him as soon as the rehearsal ended—a full scholarship to play baseball. She could hardly wait to tell him. And if he chose not to do another show, that would be fine by her, as long as he got to do the things he longed to do, develop the gifts he wanted to develop. But, for now, the boy was going to play a chicken, whether the idea settled well with him or not.

Minutes later, Tangie and Gregg prayed with the kids. Then it was time for the rehearsal to begin. Darla, who'd been looking a little pale today, sat at the piano, ready to play the intro music. The song sounded great. At the end of it, Tangie turned to Gregg and gave him a thumbs-up. He responded with a smile.

At this point, Margaret Sanderson moved to center stage, dressed as a baby chick, ready to deliver her opening lines. Her expression was clean, and her lines were flawless. However, a couple of the kids who followed bumbled theirs pretty badly. Tangie stopped the rehearsal to say something to the cast.

"Kids, I told you we would be *lines off* today."

Cody raised his hand. "What does lines off mean?"

Tangie groaned. "It means you can't use your scripts anymore. The lines are supposed to be memorized."

A round of "Oooh's" went up from the cast, and Tangie slapped herself in the head. She should've explained the term.

"How many of you know your lines?" she asked.

Annabelle and Margaret raised their hands.

"Anyone else?"

A couple of others half-raised theirs. Tangie sighed, then went back to directing the rehearsal. When it came time for Annabelle to sing her solo, Tangie breathed a sigh of relief. Surely this would redeem the day. Or not. Ironically, Annabelle sounded a little. . .strange.

"Everything okay, honey?" Tangie asked, trying not to overreact.

The child pointed to her throat. "I feel a little scratchy, and it hurts when I swallow."

"Oh no." Tangie shook her head. "Well, have your mom talk with me after the rehearsal." She would tell her to have Annabelle gargle with warm salt water and drink hot tea with lemon. Tricks of the trade for actors who'd overused their voices. In the meantime, they'd better get back to work. The show must go on, after all!

❧

Gregg watched Tangie at work, his heart heavy. With just one week till the production, he had to face the inevitable. She would be leaving him soon, going back to New York. Every fiber of his being cried out for her to stay, but he would never suggest it. No, he of all people understood what it meant to respond to the call of God. If the Lord was calling Tangie to New York, she had to go.

On the other hand, the whole New York thing might just be a distraction, right? Should he mention that? Maybe if he told her that he loved her. . .

No. He wouldn't do that. If she stayed, he wanted it to be because the Lord had spoken, not because Gregg had spoken.

But I do love her.

As he watched her work with the children, he realized his feelings—once small—had grown into a wildfire. Listening to the sound in her voice as she soothed Cody's ruffled feathers. Watching her as she diligently poured into Margaret's life, in spite of the youngster's attitude. Observing the way she continued to nurture the gifts in little Annabelle's life.

Yes, Tangie was truly one of the most amazing women he'd ever met, and easy to love.

But he couldn't tell her. Not yet, anyway.

nineteen

Two days before the show, Tangie received a phone call from Annabelle's mother. She could tell by the sound of her voice that something was amiss.

"I'm afraid our little lamb is really sick," Annabelle's mom explained.

"No! What's happened?"

"I don't know. It started out as some sort of virus, I guess. I did everything you said. She gargled with warm salt water and drank hot tea. We've been loading her up on vitamin C and even making her drink orange juice, which she doesn't like. But every day is worse than the day before. What started out as a scratchy throat is now full-blown laryngitis. She can't speak a word."

"Yikes." Tangie wanted to dive into one of those, "Oh, man! What are we going to do now?" speeches, but stopped herself short of doing so. *It's not about the show,* she reminded herself. *It's about the kids.*

Instead of saying too much, she simply offered up a few kind words. "Please tell Annabelle how sorry I am. I hope she feels better."

"I will. And please don't give her part away just yet. We're going to keep her home from school for the next two days, so I'm hoping that will help," Mrs. Lawrence said. "But I wanted to let you know so that you can begin to look for an understudy. . .just in case."

"Right. Good idea."

As she ended the phone conversation, Tangie's mind reeled. An understudy? At this late date? Which of the children was savvy enough to pick up the role this late in the game?

Really, only one person made sense. But Tangie would have to eat a little crow to make this work. She picked up the phone and punched in Margaret Sanderson's number. The child's mother answered on the third ring.

"Mrs. Sanderson, this is Tangie Carini from the church."

"Yes?"

"I, um, have a little problem and I'm hoping you and Margaret can help me with it."

"Oh?" She could read the curiosity in the woman's voice. "What's happened?"

Tangie went on to explain the predicament, finally asking to speak to Margaret. When the child came on the phone, she listened quietly, and then responded with words that stunned Tangie. "But Annabelle needs to do her part! She's the best at it. Her song is bee-*you*-tee-ful!"

Tangie laughed. "You're right. It is."

"How can I be the narrator and the littlest sheep, too?" Margaret asked.

"Oh, that's easy. The narrator costume covers you from head to toe. It's also very tall, so you look bigger in it. The little sheep costume is completely different. I don't think the audience will even realize it's the same person."

"So, you're saying I get to do both parts?" Margaret's voice began to tremble. "Both? Not just one?"

"If Annabelle can't be there, yes."

"Mom! Guess what!" Margaret hollered. "They want me to do two different parts." She returned to the phone, sounding a little breathless. "But I don't know Annabelle's song. Not very well, I mean."

"Can you meet me at the church in an hour? We'll go over it then."

"Okay. I'll ask my mom." The youngster hollered once again, finally returning to the phone with, "She says it's fine. We'll see you in an hour." After a pause, Margaret said, "Oh, and Miss Tangie. . ."

"Yes, honey?"

"I hope Annabelle gets to do her part. I'm fine with the narrator. Really I am."

Tangie smiled all the way to her toes. "Oh, honey, I'm so proud of you. And I have to tell you, you're doing an awesome job with your part. I couldn't be prouder."

As she ended the call, Tangie realized just how true those words were. Margaret had come such a long way. Then again, they'd all come a long way.

Oh, but what a great distance they had left to go!

&

Gregg sat on a barstool at the bakery, chatting with his mom as she made some of her famous homemade cinnamon rolls.

"Mom, can I ask you a question?"

"Sure, son." She continued her work, but glanced up at him with a smile. "What's up?"

"I love you so much, but I'm worried about you."

"I know you are, but I'm going to be just fine."

"Still, with all you're going through, why don't you just sell off this place? Kick back and relax a little? You deserve it."

"W–what?" She looked at him, a horrified expression on her face. "Close down Sweet Harmony? But why?"

"The shop has brought in all of the money you could need to retire in style." He shrugged. "You could live stress-free for the rest of your life. I think it would be good for you. All of this work is. . .well, it's work. And Josh and I want you to be able to take it easy."

"But honey, I'm only sixty-one. I'm not ready to retire yet. Besides. . ." Her eyes filled with tears. "Coming here every morning gives me a reason to get out of bed. People need me. And I need this shop. It's. . ." She shook her head. "It's keeping me going. I'm surprised you can't see that."

Immediately, shame washed over Gregg. He'd never considered the fact that his mom would respond with such passion. "Ah. I'm sorry I brought it up. We just want the best for you, I promise."

"I know you do, honey, but this *is* the best for me. If I keep my body busy, then my mind stays busy, too. If my mind stays busy, then there's no time left over to. . ."

"To worry?"

"Yes." She nodded, then stretched out the dough for the cinnamon rolls, adding cinnamon, sugar, and butter before rolling them. "It's all part of this great plan I've got for getting through this. Keep working. That's the answer."

"Working helps keep your mind occupied," he said. "But Mom, there's really only one answer to getting through this, and it has nothing to do with work. It's—"

"No lectures, Greggy." She turned to him with a warning look in her eye. "We've been through this. I don't mind hearing you talk about all of the things this God of yours has done for you, but I've managed pretty well without Him for the first sixty years of my life and I'll do just fine for the next sixty."

She gave him a wink, but it didn't ease the pain in his heart. What could he do to get through to her?

Just love her, Gregg. Just keep on loving her.

twenty

The afternoon of the final dress rehearsal, Tangie's nerves were a jumbled mess. The kids somehow made it through the show, but there were problems all over the place. Margaret seemed really unsure of herself in Annabelle's part, so she dropped quite a few lines. Darla wasn't feeling well, so Gregg had to play the piano in her place. The set was still incomplete, and some of the costumes still needed work. Tangie didn't know when she'd ever been more stressed or *less* ready to pull off a show.

As the rehearsal continued, Tangie offered up a plea to the Lord for both His mercies and His favor. She also spent a lot of time muttering "The show must go on" under her breath.

The rehearsal ended soon enough and Tangie prayed with the children, then handed out flyers with instructions for tomorrow's curtain call. She went over her notes one last time before releasing them. "Be here an hour before curtain. Have your hair and makeup done ahead of time. Get into costume immediately upon arrival. Meet in the choir room for vocal warm-up and prayer. Do everything you're told to do when you're told to do it."

"I'm never gonna remember all of that stuff," Cody muttered.

"That's why I've given you the flyer," Tangie explained. "Just make sure your parents read it. Oh, and kids. . .spend some time praying for our performance and for the people who will come to see it. That's the most important thing we can do."

That last part hit her especially hard. There would be people in the audience who didn't normally attend church. Some who had never heard the gospel message before. Would they really see the heart of the Good Shepherd shining through in her little play? Could a silly production about bunnies and baby chicks touch people's lives?

Suddenly, she wasn't so sure. All of her confidence faded away, leaving behind only doubt.

As they rose from their places on the stage, Tangie used her most animated stage voice to holler, "Break a leg!"

Cody, who'd taken off running the other direction, turned back to look at her with a questioning look on his face. "Huh?"

Tangie hollered out, "Cody, be careful! The set pieces still aren't finished and I don't want you to—" She never got to say the words "hurt yourself." Cody tripped over a piece of wood behind one of the flats and down it came on top of him, the canvas ripping straight in half.

He stood silent and still in the middle of the torn piece, his eyes as wide as saucers. All around the other children froze in place.

"I'm sorry, Miss Tangie." He groaned and slapped himself in the head. "But I told you I'm no good at this. I don't belong on the stage." He rubbed his ankle. "Besides, you *told* me to break my leg."

Tangie groaned, then rushed to his side to make sure he was okay. Convinced he was, she finally dismissed him. Ready to turn her attention to the ripped backdrop, she switched gears. With Gramps' help, they would get the rest of the set pieces ready before the show.

Less than a minute into the process, she heard her grandmother's voice ring out.

"Tangerine! Yoo-hoo!"

She looked up as Gran-Gran approached the stage, carrying a small box. "I, um, need to talk with you about these programs, honey." She handed one to Tangie, who looked at the cover and smiled.

"Oh, they turned out great."

"Yes and no."

"Yes and no?" Tangie looked at the cover again.

"Well, open one and see what I mean."

Tangie opened the program, realizing right away the text on the inside was upside-down. "Oh, yikes."

"The printer sends his apologies," Gran-Gran said with a shrug.

"Can't he redo them?"

"Unfortunately, he has a big order for another church in town and doesn't have time. But there's some good news."

Tangie handed the program back to her grandmother. "I could use some good news, trust me."

"He gave them to us for half price."

"Well, yippee." Tangie sighed. "I guess we don't have much choice, do we?"

"Look at the bright side. . ." Gran-Gran paused for a few seconds, her brow wrinkled.

"What's that?" Tangie asked.

"I'm trying to think of one." Her grandmother laughed. "But nothing's coming to me."

Tangie knelt to fix the torn backdrop, seaming the backside with heavy tape. However, just a few minutes into it, she heard Gregg's voice ring out from the auditorium. "Tangie, I hate to tell you this. You have no idea how much I hate to tell you this." He climbed the steps to the stage.

With exhaustion eking from every pore, Tangie looked up at him. "What's happened now?"

"It's Darla."

Tangie's heart quickened. "Darla?" She put down the roll of tape and looked into Gregg's eyes. "What's happened to her? She hasn't been in an accident or anything, has she?"

"No, nothing like that." Gregg shook his head. "It's her appendix. They've taken her to surgery to remove it. Doctor says if they'd waited another day it could've been deadly."

"No! Oh, Gregg." Tangie crumpled onto the floor, and

the tears started. "What are we going to do? How in the world can we pull this off without Darla? We can't have live music without a musician." On and on she went, bemoaning the fact that the show couldn't possibly go on without the pianist.

Finally, when she regained control of her senses, Tangie sighed. "I'm so sorry. That was completely heartless. I should be saying how bad I feel for Darla, and instead I'm thinking only of myself."

"Well, not only of yourself." Gregg gave her a sympathetic look. "You're thinking of the kids. And the parents. And the other musicians. And the audience. And then, maybe, at the bottom of the list, yourself."

"Right." Tangie shook her head, then whispered, "I give up."

"W—what?"

"You heard me." She looked at him, determination setting in. "I give up. I can't do this. I'm not cut out to handle this much pressure."

"B—but. . .whatever happened to 'The show must go on'? Doesn't that stand for anything?"

"There's a time to admit defeat, Gregg, and this is it. Our leading lady has laryngitis, our set is in pieces, Cody very nearly broke his leg when he tripped earlier, the programs are upside-down, and now Darla can't be here to play the piano for the show."

"Anything else?"

"Yes." She stared at him with tears now flowing. "The drama director is having a nervous breakdown!"

He joined her on the floor and opened his arms to comfort her, but she wasn't having any of it. No, sir. Not today. Today she just wanted everyone to go away and leave her alone.

❧

Gregg watched all of this, completely mesmerized. First of all, he'd never seen a grown woman throw a tantrum like this before. He found it almost comical. Entertaining, at the very least. Still, he did his best to hide any hint of a smile. Might just send Tangie over the edge. Looked like she was pretty close already.

twenty-one

On the Saturday of the big show, Tangie was a nervous wreck. Before she left for the church, she spent some time praying. Only the Lord could pull this off.

She rode to the church with her grandparents, script in hand. Nestled beside her on the back car seat, the box holding the football-sized chocolate egg. Taffie had sent it, along with a note reading, BREAK A LEG. Tangie was half tempted to pick up the phone and tell her about Cody's mishap. Maybe she'd have time for that later. Right now, they had a show to put on.

After the Easter egg hunt, anyway.

She arrived at the church to find Ashley and other children's workers hard at work, putting out Easter eggs in designated areas, according to the ages of the children. Tangie looked at her with a smile. "How's it going?"

Ashley smiled. "Great!" She drew near and whispered, "Have you heard my news?"

"News?" Tangie shifted her script to the other arm and shook her head. "What is it?"

Ashley displayed her left hand, wiggling her ring finger so that there would be no doubt. A sparkling diamond adorned that finger, nestled into a beautiful white-gold setting.

"Oh, Ashley! You're engaged?"

When she nodded, Tangie's joy turned to sorrow. "Does. . . does that mean you're leaving?"

"Nah. Paul and I have talked about it. He has his own web-design business. He can do that here, in Harmony. So, it looks like we'll settle in here, raise a family. You know." She gave Tangie a wink.

Tangie's stomach tumbled to her toes. *She's assuming that's what Gregg and I will do, too. But I'll be in New York, not Harmony.*

Tangie forced her thoughts back to the present. "I'm thrilled for you!" After a few more words of congratulations, she heard Gregg's voice sound from behind her. Tangie turned around, smiling as she caught a glimpse of him.

"Ready for the big day?" he asked, drawing near.

"As ready as I'll ever be." She sighed, and he gave her an inquisitive look.

"What?"

"Well, I guess I should just admit that you were right all along. Doing a play with kids is a lot tougher than it looks. And all of the Broadway experience in the world didn't prepare me for this."

Ashley laughed. "Nothing can prepare you for the chaos of kids, but they're worth it."

"They are."

"And I heard there's some good news where Annabelle's concerned," Gregg said.

"Yes." Tangie grinned. "Her mom called this morning and said she's got her voice back. Said it was a miracle. When Annabelle went to bed last night things weren't any better. But this morning. . ."

"Was a brand-new day." Ashley laughed. "Oh, God is good, isn't He?"

"He is." Tangie smiled—and all the more as guests started arriving. Within the hour, the whole church property was alive with activity. She had never seen so many children. And the Easter baskets! Nearly every child held one.

Except the kids in the production, of course. They hadn't come to hunt for Easter eggs. They were here to do a show.

Tangie glanced at her watch. One o'clock. Time to meet with the cast and crew in the choir room for final instructions. She and Gregg made their way inside, finding a lively crowd waiting for them. She managed to get the kids quieted down, and Gregg opened in prayer. Then he nodded for Tangie to begin.

"Kids, I know you've missed out on some of the activities outside," she told them with a playful smile, "but it will be worth it when that auditorium fills up with neighborhood kids."

Cody raised his hand. "My best friend is here. I already told him I'm wearing a chicken suit and he didn't laugh, so I don't think I'll have to give him a black eye or anything."

"Well, that's nice." Tangie stifled a laugh.

Annabelle's hand went up, too. "My aunt came and she brought my cousins. They've never been in a church before. My mom says it's kind of like a miracle."

Tangie's heart swelled with joy. "It is like a miracle." *Lord, You're proving what I've said all along. . .the arts are a great way to reach out to people who don't know You. Use this production, Father. Reach those who haven't heard the gospel message before.*

"Kids, let's pray before we do the show." Tangie instructed them to stand and get into a circle. Some of the boys were a little hesitant to join hands, but eventually they formed a large, unified ring. At this point, she encouraged the children to pray, not just for the show, but also for those in attendance. By the end of the prayer time, Tangie had tears in her eyes. For that matter, Gregg did, too. From across the room, she gave him a wink, then mouthed the words, "Break a leg." He nodded, then ushered the children toward the stage.

❧

Gregg took his seat at the piano, stretched his arms, and then whispered a prayer that all would go well. He could take Darla's place as chief musician, ensuring the show would go on, but that was where his role ended. Everything from this point forth was up to the Lord. Would He take the little bit they'd given Him and use it to His glory? Only time would tell.

The lights went down in the auditorium, but not before Gregg saw his mother slip in the back door. He whispered a quiet, "Thank You, Lord," then began to play the opening number.

The stage lights came up, and the colorful set came alive. The colors had seemed bright before, but not like this. Maybe it was the energy of the crowd. There were, after all, over three hundred elementary aged children in the room. Everything seemed brighter and happier.

In the center of the stage, the spotlight hit the giant Easter egg. Then, as the music progressed, the egg began to crack from the inside out. "Good girl, Margaret," he whispered. "Come on out of that protective shell of pride you've been wearing. Show 'em what you've got."

She did just that. As she emerged dressed as a baby chick, the audience came alive with laughter and joy. "It's a chicken!" one little girl hollered.

Not swayed, Margaret delivered her line with perfection. Then Annabelle entered the stage. Oh, how cute she looked in that little lamb costume. Tangie had been right. The kids loved this sort of thing. Annabelle opened her mouth to sing, and a holy hush fell over the audience. In fact, by the end of the song, Gregg could hardly see the keys. His eyes were, after all, filled with tears.

ᴥ

When the show ended, Tangie rushed around backstage, congratulating the children and thanking them for doing such a terrific job. When the last of the kids had finally gone, she plopped down into a chair, completely dumbfounded. "You did it, Lord. You pulled it off." And, with the exception of a couple of minor glitches, the show had been as close to perfect as any show could be. "Lord, I believe in miracles. I've just witnessed one." She paused for a moment to think of all He had done. More than anything else, the Lord had convinced Tangie that she did, indeed, have a call on her life to work with kids. Maybe it hadn't always been easy. . .but it had been worth it. No doubt about that.

"A penny for your thoughts." Tangie looked up as she heard a familiar voice. Gregg's mom stood in front of her, a broad smile on her face. "I liked your bunny show."

Tangie laughed. "Seriously?"

"Seriously. Lots to chew on. I'll have to get back with you on all of that. But I wanted you to know I think you and Gregg did an awesome job." Penny leaned down and whispered, "And didn't he sound great on the piano?"

"He sure did. You should hear him on Sundays. He's the best." Tangie stopped herself from saying more. Didn't want to push the envelope. Still, Penny was right. Gregg had saved the day by stepping into the role of pianist.

Penny glanced at her watch. "Well, I've got to scoot. Thank goodness Sarah was home from school and could babysit the store for me this afternoon."

"I'm so glad." Tangie smiled.

"You coming in on Monday?" Penny asked. "There's going to be a lot of cleanup."

Tangie gave a hesitant nod. "M—maybe. I'll get back to you on that."

Penny nodded, but took off in a hurry.

Tangie rose and started cleaning up the stage area. As she reached the farthest corner, a couple of familiar voices rang out.

"Tangerine!"

She turned, stunned to see her sisters and their husbands standing there. "Taffie? Candy!" Tangie sprinted their way, her heart now beating double-time as she saw her little niece cradled in Taffie's arms. "What are you doing here?"

"You didn't think Gran-Gran would let us get away with not seeing the show, did you?" Candy said, her words framed in laughter.

"And besides, I wanted Callie to see her Aunt Tangie in her first church performance," Taffie added, passing the darling baby girl off to Tangie.

She held the beautiful infant, her heart suddenly quite full. "Did you come alone, or. . ."

"Oh, you mean Mom and Dad?" Candy shrugged. "They're in Texas this week. But Mom sends her love. And Dad says—"

"Break a leg!" they all shouted in unison.

"So, you saw the show?" Tangie gave her sisters a hesitant look. When they nodded, she asked, "W–what did you think?"

"You're kidding, right?" Candy shook her head. "It was amazing, Tangie. I got it. Every bit of symbolism. Every nuance. It was all there. And the kids were amazing."

"So was their director," Taffie added with a wink.

"Yes, you're a natural," Candy agreed as she reached to give her a hug. "You were born for the theater." She said the word *theater* in an exaggerated British accent, making everyone laugh.

Tangie wanted to ask her sisters' opinion, whether she should—or shouldn't—go to New York to audition for *A Woman in Love*. But this wasn't the time. No, this was the time to cuddle her niece, chat with her sisters. . .and introduce everyone to one very special music director.

twenty-two

The Monday after the big show, Tangie received a call from a very hyper Marti.

"You're coming home, right? Vincent called again, and he said to tell you to be at the Marlowe Theater at two o'clock on Wednesday afternoon. That's the final day of the auditions. In my opinion, it's better to go last than first. You'll leave a lasting impression on him that way."

"I guess." Tangie sighed. "I've been praying about it, Marti, but I'm just not sure." Every time she prayed, images of Gregg's face popped up in front of her. And the children. . . she would miss them something fierce. She would miss Penny, too. And her grandparents. Would it really be worth it—to trade in the people she now loved. . .for a production?

"We're not talking forever," Marti reminded her. "It's just one show. And what can it hurt to audition? You don't have to bring all of your stuff when you come. Just bring a bag or two. Come tomorrow and stay at my place for a few days. You can make your decision after you get here. If you get the part, maybe that will be a sign you're supposed to be back here. If you don't. . ." Marti paused. "Well, I don't want to think about that because I really want you back in New York. But you can decide for yourself, okay?"

"Okay." Tangie realized this was really the only thing that made sense. If she didn't go back to New York and audition for this role, she'd never know for sure whether she belonged in the Big Apple or in Harmony. And, if she didn't at least give this a shot, she'd never know if she had what it took to be a leading lady.

Tangie settled down onto the bed, reaching for one of the

programs from the children's musical. The kids had signed it—using their childish scribbles to offer up their thanks for the role she'd played. She grinned as she saw Cody's signature, followed by, *Break a Leg!* And then there was Annabelle's childish script, followed by, *Thank you for believing in me.* Her favorite, however, was Margaret's. After the beautiful, well-placed signature, the tempestuous little girl had written, *This was the best play ever! Thanks for letting me be the narrator!*

"Lord, I'm going to miss these kids. And my grandparents. And. . ."

She sighed. Most of all, she would miss Gregg. She'd miss the look of disbelief in his eyes when she said something outlandish. She'd miss the way they harmonized together. Most of all, she'd miss the way he looked deep into her soul, challenging her to be a better person.

Determined to get through this, Tangie made her way to the living room. She found her grandparents watching TV.

"I, um, I need to talk to you."

"Not now, honey." Her grandmother shooed her away with the wave of a hand. "We're watching *The Price is Right.*"

"Yes, but. . .I need to tell you something."

Gran-Gran looked up, and for the first time Tangie noticed the tears in her eyes. "We know you do, honey. But not right now." The way her grandmother emphasized the last four words stopped Tangie cold.

Ah ha. She just doesn't want to face the fact that I'm leaving. Well, fine. I'll talk to them later. Right now, she needed to head over to Sweet Harmony to let Penny know about her decision. Then, of course, she had to talk to Gregg.

Every time she thought about telling him, Tangie felt a lump in her throat. The sting of tears burned her eyes. She'd fallen for him. No doubt about that. But then again, she always fell for the leading man. Right? What made this one different from the others?

She drove to town, noticing, for the first time, the green

leaves bursting through on the trees. "Oh, Lord! I've been so busy with the show I almost missed it! Spring!"

Yes, everywhere she looked, the radiant colors of spring greeted her. They were in the blue waters of the little creek on the outskirts of town. They were in the tender white blossoms in the now-budding pear trees. Even the cars seemed more colorful than before, now that they weren't covered in dirty snow.

Yes, color had come to Harmony at the very time she had to leave.

"Stop it, Tangie. It's springtime in New York, too." She forced her thoughts to Manhattan as she pulled her car into the parking lot at Sweet Harmony. By the time she climbed out of the car, Tangie had a new resolve. "I can do this. What's the big deal, anyway?"

She pushed open the front door of the bakery, the bell jangling its usual welcome. Tangie drew in a deep breath and approached Penny, who was working behind the counter.

"Well, hey, kiddo. I wondered if you might come in today. Made up your mind yet? Are you staying or going?"

Talk about cutting to the chase. Penny was never one to mince words. Well, fine. She wouldn't either. "Penny, I hate to tell you this, but. . ."

"You're leaving for New York."

"Yes."

Penny set down the mound of dough she'd been kneading and gave Tangie a pensive look. "Well, look, kid, I've been preparing myself for it for weeks. I'll just put a sign in the window, and—"

"No, please don't do that. Not yet anyway." Tangie's nerves kicked in. "I'm going to New York, but I don't know if I'm going to stay. Auditions are on Wednesday, so I need to leave tomorrow. I should know something a few days later. Can you give me a week, Penny? I'll call if I'm not coming back."

"Sure." With the wave of a hand, Penny dismissed the idea.

"I'll get Josh to help me till then. It won't hurt the boy to work with his mama. Go on and go to that audition. Might do you some good." She went to work washing out one of the mixing bowls. " 'Course, if you stay in New York it'll break our hearts, but don't fret over that." She turned back and gave Tangie a wink. "Kidding, kiddo. You chase after your dreams."

"Thank you for understanding, Penny. I'm praying about what to do, but God hasn't really given me a clear answer." She glanced down at the tattoo on her wrist, pondering the little star. *Is this really where I'm supposed to go, God? To follow that star? To see where it leads me?*

Everything in Penny's demeanor changed at the mention of the word *God*. Her happy-go-lucky smile faded, and she exhaled. Loudly.

"What?" Tangie approached with a bit of hesitation.

"Well, since you brought up God and all. . ." Penny began to fidget.

"What about Him?"

"I just wanted to tell you something. I've been thinking a lot about this. That play you and Gregg put on with the kids. . . it was, well, it was great."

"Really?" Tangie's heart wanted to burst into song with this news.

Penny's eyes filled with tears. "This is going to sound nuts, but that scene where the little sheep has the conversation with the shepherd about wandering away from the fold. . ." Penny's eyes misted over. "I got it, Tangie. I understood what you were trying to say. I'm that little sheep."

"Yes." A lump rose in Tangie's throat, and she could hardly contain her emotions. "T–that's right."

"Let me ask you a question. Did you write that play with me in mind?"

Tangie smiled. "To be completely honest, no. I just wrote it with *people* in mind. God loves people, Penny. All people. And He desires that we love Him back. It's really pretty simple. That's why I used such a childlike platform to get that message across."

"So childlike an old fool like me could get it." Penny smiled as she gazed into Tangie's eyes. "Oh, by the way, thanks for letting Josh play the role of the shepherd. I haven't seen him this excited since I gave him that *Star Wars* lunch box in the second grade."

Tangie laughed. "He did a great job. And I think memorizing those lines about how much God loves His kids really did something to him."

"I think you're right." After a moment, Penny's brow wrinkled. "Seeing God as a shepherd really messed up my thinking, I'll have you know."

"It did?"

"Yes." Penny exhaled, pursed her lips, then said, "I never saw Him as kindhearted or loving before. I guess I always figured God was as mean-spirited as some of the people who say they represent Him."

"He's not." Tangie shook her head. "And I'm sorry your experience with the church was painful. I can only tell you that the people I know who love the Lord are just the opposite of what you've described. They're loving and giving, and they accept people, no matter what." She gestured to her bright red hair, her tattoos, and then the tiny diamond stud in her nose. "I speak from experience. No one there has ever judged me."

"Except me."

The male voice sounded behind her, and Tangie turned to find Gregg standing there. He must've slipped in the back door, but when?

"W—what?" Tangie turned to face him.

"I judged you." He sighed. "I don't think I did it on purpose, but I'm pretty sure I didn't give you a fair shake in the beginning. I'm not sure why."

"My appearance?" she asked.

"I don't know. I think it's just that we're so opposite. It took me awhile to adjust to the fact that I'd be working with someone who's my polar opposite."

"You two are about as different as singing rabbits and dancing chickens," his mother threw in. "But that's what makes relationships so interesting."

"Yes, opposites do attract." He took Tangie's hands in his and stared into her eyes. "But the real question is, can this relationship stand the test of time?"

&

Gregg's heart *thump-thumped* so loudly, he could hear it in his ears. He'd walked in at just the right moment—or maybe just the wrong moment, depending on how you looked at it. Tangie was leaving. She'd confirmed it. And he wouldn't stop her, though everything within him rebelled at the idea of losing her.

And all of that stuff his mom had said to Tangie about the play. Had she really come face-to-face with the Good Shepherd, thanks to a kids' Easter production? If so, then God had truly worked a miracle.

His mom gave him a wink, then disappeared into the back room. Gregg took this as his cue. He wrapped Tangie in his arms, thankful there were no customers in the store.

"So, you're leaving tomorrow?" he whispered, leaning in to press a kiss onto her cheek.

"I am." She lingered in his arms, giving him hope.

He reached to brush a loose hair from her face.

"I'll never know what might've happened if I don't go."

"I understand. And I support you. It's killing me, but I support you."

Tangie gave him a playful pout. "You'll wait for me?"

"Wait for you? Hmm." He paused a moment, just to make her wonder, then grinned. "Till the end of time."

"Very dramatic. Spoken like a true theater person." Tangie winked, then kissed the tip of his nose.

He wanted to grab her and give her a kiss convincing enough to stay put, but the bell above the bakery door jangled. A customer walked in. At that same moment, Gregg's mother reappeared from the back room.

"You two lovebirds need to go build your nest elsewhere." His mom snapped a dishtowel at him. "I'm trying to run a business here."

"Mm-hmm." He nodded, gingerly letting go of Tangie's hands.

"I need to get to work, anyway," Tangie said, reaching for an apron. "This is going to be my last day. . .for a while, anyway."

"Last day." Gregg swallowed hard and settled onto a barstool. If this was her last day, he wanted to spend every minute of it with her.

"Oh, but, Gregg, before I go." She turned to him with a winning smile. "There is one little thing you need to do."

"Oh?"

"Yes." She nodded, a hint of laughter in her eyes. "I seem to remember someone once promising he would eat a whole plateful of artichokes in front of the kids if the performance went well."

Gregg groaned, remembering. "You're going to hold me to that?"

"I am." Tangie nodded. "And, in fact, it might just be the thing that woos me back to Harmony. I'd pay money to see you eat artichokes."

"What? Artichokes?" Penny laughed. "This boy of mine can't stand artichokes."

"I know, I know." Gregg sighed. Still, he had promised. And Tangie had given him hope with her last statement, anyway. Maybe she would come back to Harmony. When the time was right. For that, he would eat all the artichokes in the state of New Jersey.

twenty-three

Tangie made the drive to New York, her mind going a hundred different directions. She arrived in short order, marveling at the noise and fast-paced chaos she found. Had it always been this crazy?

Seeing Marti was such a thrill. They spent Tuesday afternoon visiting all of their favorite places—Hanson's Deli, the art museum, FAO Schwarz, and Macy's, of course.

On Wednesday morning, Tangie shifted gears. Before she even climbed out of bed, she ushered up a lengthy prayer, asking for God's will. She wouldn't dare make a move outside of it, not with so much at stake.

At one thirty, she caught a cab to the Marlowe Theater. At a quarter of two, she walked through the back doors into the familiar auditorium. At once, her heart came alive. Oh, how she'd missed this place! It captivated her, set something aflame inside of her.

She filled out an audition form, reached into her bag for her music and resume, and passed everything off to Vincent's assistant, a girl named Catherine. Then, when her name was called, Tangie walked to the center of the stage, ready to audition. She drew in a deep breath and sent one last silent prayer heavenward. Then the music began.

With as much confidence as she could muster, she sang the first few lines from "On My Own," one of her personal favorites. Closing her eyes, she allowed the melody to consume her. It felt so good to be back on the stage. And that Vincent hadn't cut the song short yet. That was a good sign.

Not only did he *not* cut her short, she actually sang the entire piece. When the music drew to a close, Tangie smiled in his direction. Even with the stage lights in her eyes, she could see the contented look in his eye. So far, so good.

"We'd like to hear you read, please," he said.

Catherine crossed the stage with a script in hand, which she passed off to Tangie.

"Start at the top of page 4 and read for Gina," Vincent said. "We're going to bring in one of the guys to read against you."

He looked around the empty auditorium and then shrugged. "What happened to our guys?"

Catherine gasped. "I'm sorry, Vincent. I really thought you said you were done with the guys until callbacks."

"Did I? I can't remember."

Tangie shrugged. "I can just read both parts if you like. Or maybe you could call out Harrison's lines."

Just then, a noise at the back of the auditorium startled her. With the stage lights in her eyes, she could barely make out the figure of a man walking down the aisle toward the stage.

Vincent rose and greeted him. "Perfect timing. You'll need to stand center stage next to this beautiful young woman to read for Harrison."

The man stopped, and Tangie squinted to see him better. Was. . .was that. . .? No, it couldn't possibly be.

Just then, a familiar voice rang out. "You. . .you want me to read for a part?"

Gregg!

"Isn't that what you're here for?" The director sounded a little perturbed.

His voice rang out loud and clear. "Oh, well, actually I. . ." He climbed the steps leading to the stage and for the first time, came into full view.

Tangie gasped as she saw him. "Gregg, w–what are you doing here?"

"I. . ." He squinted against the bright lights, then put his hand over his eyes.

"He's here to audition for Harrison," the director said, the impatience evident in his voice. The older man climbed the steps to the stage and pressed a script into Gregg's hand. "Top of page 4. Read Harrison's lines. We'll listen to you sing afterward."

"E–Excuse me?" Gregg's face paled, and the script now bobbed up and down in his trembling hand.

"Just do what he says," Tangie whispered. "Please."

Gregg looked down at the script, then began to read the lines, sounding a little stilted " 'Gina, I don't know any other way to say it. I've told you a hundred times in a hundred different ways. I love you.' " He looked up from the script, his eyes wide.

Tears filled Tangie's eyes as she took his hand in hers and read her line. " 'Sometimes we only see what we want to see. It's so hard to crack through that protective shell we all wear. So, maybe you've been saying it, but I didn't hear it. Does that make sense?' "

" 'Perfect sense.' " Gregg looked up from the script as he continued. " 'Sometimes we resist the very thing that's meant to be because it's different from what we're used to, or because we're afraid.' "

Tangie almost laughed aloud at the words. *Lord, what are You doing here?* Her hand trembled in Gregg's, but it had nothing to do with the audition.

He tossed the script on the stage and stared at her. "Tangie, I've been the world's biggest fool."

"Wait, that's not in the script!" the director hollered out.

"I should have told you that I loved you before you left. I drove all the way here just to say it." Gregg spoke with deeper passion than Tangie had ever heard before. Tears covered his lashes as the words poured out. "I don't know what took me so long. Guess I let fear get in the way."

"That makes two of us," she whispered, her voice filled with emotion. "I've been afraid to say it, too." The script slipped out of her hands and clattered to the floor.

"We're as different as night and day, just like my mom said. But, you are who you were born to be," he responded, taking both of her hands in his. "And so am I. But being without you these past two days has almost killed me. I can't eat. I can't sleep. I can't even play the piano anymore. Everything in me stopped functioning when you left, and I don't know what I can do to make things normal again."

Tangie smiled and squeezed his hand. "Oh, we're halfway to normal already, trust me."

He took her in his arms and cupped her chin in his palm. Such tenderness poured out of his eyes. She'd never known such powerful emotions.

"I love you, Tangie. I love every quirky, wonderful, unique thing about you. I love that you're different."

"Hey, now—"

"In a wonderful, glorious sort of way. And I love that you love me, even though I'm just a boring, predictable guy." He leaned into her, a passionate kiss following his words.

For a moment, time seemed to hang suspended. All that mattered was this man. *He loves me!* Tangie whispered the words, "*That* wasn't boring," in his ear, then giggled.

They lingered in each other's arms, whispering words of sweetness. Until a voice rang out.

"Best version of that scene I've seen all day. Where have you two been all my life?"

Tangie opened her eyes, suddenly blinded by the stage lights. Squinting, she made out the face of the director. "Oh my goodness." How could she possibly make Vincent understand. . .they weren't acting!

"I love the way you took the lines and made them your own." The older man spoke in a gravelly voice. "Brilliant. No one else has taken the time to do it. And there's a chemistry between the two of you that's. . .well, wowza! We don't see a lot of that. People can act like they're in love, of course, but to actually pull off a convincing love scene? Almost impossible."

Tangie laughed until she couldn't see straight. Gregg joined her, of course. The only one who wasn't laughing was Vincent.

"I'm glad you think this is so funny," he said. "You're going to have to clue me in on whatever I've missed. But in the meantime, you've got the part." He looked at Tangie, then shifted his gaze to Gregg. "And if this guy can sing half as well as he can act, he's got the part, too!"

Tangie's head began to swim, and the laughter continued. Then, quite suddenly, she stopped and looked Gregg in the eye. "Let me ask you a question."

"Shoot."

"You once said that I had issues with leading ladies, that I was secretly jealous of them."

Gregg groaned. "I wish I could take that back. I'm so sorry."

"No, you're missing my point." She grinned at him. "I just need to know one thing, Gregg Burke. Do you think I'm leading lady material?"

"Always have been and always will be."

"Okay, then." She turned back to the director with a smile. "In that case, forget the play." Tangie looked at Gregg with her heart overflowing as she spoke the only words that made sense.

"This girl's going back to Harmony."

twenty-four

Tangie finished painting the set piece and stepped back to have a look at the stage. She smiled as she looked at the road sign she'd just put in place. One arrow pointed to Broadway, the other to Harmony, New Jersey. Perfect.

Gramps entered, covered in paint. "Do you think we'll get it done in time for the show? We're on at two, right?"

"Yes. Still not sure about the backdrop, though. Do you think it will be dry?"

"Won't make any difference if it's dry or not. The show must go on, honey." He walked out backstage, muttering all the while. "You're a theater person. I would think you'd know that. Doesn't matter if the set isn't built, if the costumes aren't ready, if the lines aren't memorized. The show goes on, regardless."

Tangie laughed until she couldn't see straight. *Thank You, Lord, for the reminder.*

"Honey, what are you doing in here?" Her mother's voice rang out.

"Yeah, don't you have a wedding to go to or something?" her older sister Taffie said with a laugh.

"Yes, I do." Tangie looked down at her hands and sighed as she realized they were still covered in paint. "I don't exactly look like a bride, though, do I?"

"You will soon enough," Candy said, drawing near. "But first we've got to get you into costume."

"Oh, it's no costume, trust me." Tangie sighed as she thought about the blissfully beautiful wedding dress her sisters had helped her choose. "This is one time I'm going with something traditional."

"Well, it's going to be the only thing traditional at this

wedding," Candy said, coming up the aisle. "I've never known anyone who got married at a community theater before."

"You're a fine one to talk!" Tangie laughed. "You got married on an airstrip." She turned to Taffie. "And you got married on the beach."

"I guess all of the Carini girls went a different direction on their wedding day," Candy said with a giggle. "But I still think getting married in a theater—especially one this beautiful— tops them all."

"It's the perfect way to christen the building!" Tangie looked around the theater, marveling at the changes that had occurred over the last six months. The whole thing had been Penny's doing. She'd hung posters around town, asking for the community's support. And, once the funds started rolling in, the old Bijou movie house had morphed into the most beautiful community theater ever.

The artichoke thing had been a big hit, too. Tangie didn't mind taking the credit for that one. Folks had contributed up to a hundred dollars per artichoke. Gregg had downed nearly two dozen of them, all funds going to the new theater, of course. Then again, the artichokes didn't stay down long, but that part didn't matter. The money had come in, and the old movie house was now a fabulous place for folks in the town of Harmony to put on productions.

Tangie still marveled at the transformation.

Of course, she marveled at a good many transformations, of late. Take Penny, for instance. Now that her chemo treatments were behind her, she was feeling better. So much better, in fact, that she'd joined the church. She now thrived on providing sweets for the monthly women's tea. And Tangie had it on good authority that Penny also slipped Gramps free donuts for the Prime Timers. He wasn't complaining.

No, these days Gramps had little to complain about. He was too busy working on the theater and celebrating the fact that Tangie had come back. Well, that and driving Gran-Gran back and forth to auditions. She'd reluctantly agreed to be in the community theater's first performance of *The Sound of Music*. Tangie hadn't shared the news yet, but she'd be casting her grandmother in the role of the Mother Superior. What havoc that would wreak at home!

But no time to think about productions now! Only the one at two o'clock mattered today.

Tangie stepped back, looking at the fabulous décor on the stage. "All things bright. . ."

"And beautiful," her grandmother whispered, stepping alongside her. "It's fabulous, Tangerine. You've done a great job, and this is going to be the best wedding ever."

"I do believe you're right." Tangie turned with tears in her eyes. "I do believe you're right."

❧

Gregg left the ball field at one fifteen, racing toward the theater. He hadn't wanted to miss Cody's game, of course, but there were more important things on his schedule today. His wedding, for instance.

Gregg pulled up to the theater, amazed to find so many cars out front. "Oh no. I hope I'm not later than I think." He leaped from the car, pausing to open the back door and grab his tuxedo and shoes.

When had his life become so chaotic? Where had all of the organization and structure gone? And then there was the wardrobe! These days, he was more likely to wind up wearing a chicken suit than a suit and tie.

Not that he was complaining. Oh no. Falling in love with Tangie meant falling in love with theater—lock, stock, and barrel. And there was no turning back, especially today, when he faced the performance of a lifetime.

Still, there would be no funny costumes on today's stage. They'd agreed to that. She would wear a white wedding gown—one he looked forward to seeing—and he would look top-notch in coat and tails. Bridesmaids and groomsmen would wear traditional garb, as well. No, nothing to take away from the beauty of their marriage vows or the amazing work God had done in their lives. Besides, there were sure to be costumes in abundance over the years to come.

Gregg sprinted into the theater, pausing only for a moment to look at the stage. "Whoa." Talk about a transformation. Tangie and her grandfather had done it again. Then again, she always managed to pull rabbits out of hats. Sometimes symbolically, other times for real.

Gregg reached the men's dressing area backstage, finding Josh inside, already dressed.

"You had me worried, man." Josh grinned as he ushered Gregg inside, then closed the door behind him.

"Sorry. Didn't want to miss Cody's game. You should see him, Josh. He's incredible. I think we've really discovered his true gifting."

Scrambling into his tux was the easy part. Getting the tie on was another matter. Thankfully, his mother rapped on the door just as he gave up. After he hollered, "Come in," she entered the room, her eyes filling with tears at once.

"Oh, Greggy." She shook her head. "You're quite dashing."

"Very theatrical response." He gave her a wink and she drew near to fix his tie. "I need you, Mom."

"It feels good to be needed." She worked her magic, then stepped back and sighed. "That Tangie is a lucky girl."

"No, I'm the lucky one." Gregg paused, thinking of just how blessed he felt right now. In such a short time, the Lord had brought him his perfect match—someone who also turned out to be his polar opposite. What was it Tangie had said again? That God was always at work behind the scenes, doing things they couldn't see or understand?

Lord, it's true. You saw beyond my stiff, outward appearance to my heart, and You knew I needed someone like Tangie. She's perfect for me.

He allowed his thoughts to shift to the day they'd met. . .

how she looked. What she was wearing. Then his thoughts shifted once again to that day in the diner when she'd shown up in that crazy hat. Funny, how he'd grown to love that hat over the months.

"Look at the time!"

Gregg snapped to attention at his mother's words. This was not the time for daydreams. Right now, he had a wedding to attend!

&

Tangie stood at the back of the theater, mesmerized by the crowd, the beauty of the stage, and the look of pure joy in her future husband's eyes. She thought back to her first impression of Gregg. What was it she'd told Gran-Gran, again? How had she described him over the phone that day? *"Sort of a geeky looking guy? Short hair. Looks like his mother dressed him?"*

Oh, how her impressions had changed. Then again, the Lord had changed a great many things, hadn't He? He'd washed away any preconceived ideas of how a person should look or dress and dug much deeper—to the heart of the matter. And just as she'd predicted, He'd been working in the backstage areas of her life, fine-tuning both her career and her personal life.

And what a personal life! The familiar music cued up—the theme song from *A Woman in Love*, of course—and she took her father's arm, taking steps up the long aisle toward her husband-to-be. *Just stay focused. Just stay focused.*

Somehow they made it through the ceremony, though the whole thing flew by at warp speed. She spent the time in a beautiful whirlwind of emotions.

Finally, the moment came, one she and Gregg had kept secret from their friends and family for weeks. Darla took her seat at the piano and the familiar music for *Embraceable You* began. Tangie looked at her amazing husband with a grin. She mouthed the words, "You ready?" and he nodded.

Then, the two of them joined heart, mind, and voice. . .for a harmony sweeter than the town itself.

epilogue

Ten Years Later

Tangie tucked her daughter, Guinevere, into bed and gave her a kiss on the forehead.

"So, is that the whole story, Mommy?" Gwen asked with an exaggerated sigh. "You met Daddy doing a play at the church?"

"That's right. We met doing a play, and we've done dozens of them since. . .at the church and the community theater."

"I love it when you and Daddy sing together. You sound bee-*you*-tee-ful! And your plays are so much fun. But"—the youngster's angelic face contorted into a pout—"when can *I* be in one of them?"

"Hmm, let's see." Tangie thought for a moment. "You're nearly seven now. I guess that's old enough to start acting. But only if you want to. Mommy and Daddy want you to be whatever you feel God is calling you to be."

The youngster's face lit up, and her brown eyes sparkled as she made her announcement. "I'm going to be an actress and a singer, just like Margaret Sanderson!"

Tangie had to laugh at that one. Her daughter had fallen head over heels for the community theater's newest drama director. Then again, Margaret had come a long way from that stubborn little girl who'd insisted upon getting the lead in the shows. These days, she was happier to see others promoted while she worked behind the scenes. Funny how life turned out.

"Honey, just promise me this." Tangie looked her daughter in the eye. "Promise you'll use whatever gifts God gives you to tell others about Him."

"Oh, I promise, Mommy. I'll sing about Him. . .and I'll act for Him, too." Gwen giggled.

"And if you decide you want to be a softball player or something like that. . .well, that's okay, too."

"Softball?" Gwen wrinkled her nose. "But I don't know anything about sports."

"You are your mother's daughter, for sure." Tangie laughed.

"And her father's daughter," Gregg called out as he entered the room.

Tangie looked up as her husband drew near. Her heart still did that crazy flip-flop thing, even after all these years. Oh, how she loved this man! He sat on the edge of the bed and kissed their daughter on the forehead.

"So, your mom's been telling you a bedtime story?" he asked.

"Mm-hmm." Gwen yawned. "It was the best ever, about a singing rabbit and a dancing chicken."

"I know that story well." Gregg laughed. "Did she tell you that they lived happily ever after?"

Gwen shook her head and yawned once more. "No, I think she left that part out."

Tangie smiled as she watched her daughter doze off.

Gregg rose from the bed and swept his wife into his arms. Brushing a loose hair from her face, he whispered, "You left out the happily ever after part?"

Tangie chuckled. "Well, the show's not over yet, silly. How can I give away the ending?"

"This one's a given." He kissed the end of her nose, then held her close.

As she melted into his embrace, Tangie reflected back on that day when Gregg had come to the theater in New York to tell her he loved her. On that magnificent Broadway stage—with the lights shining in their eyes—they'd tossed all scripts aside and created lines of their own, lines better than any playwright could manufacture. They were straight from the heart, words that set the rest of her life in motion. They'd sent her reeling. . .all the way back to Harmony.

And now, as she gazed into her husband's loving eyes, Tangie had to admit the truth. She knew exactly how this story would end. The singing rabbit and the dancing chicken. . . well, they would live happily ever after. Of course.

A Letter To Our Readers

Dear Reader:

In order that we might better contribute to your reading enjoyment, we would appreciate your taking a few minutes to respond to the following questions. We welcome your comments and read each form and letter we receive. When completed, please return to the following:

Fiction Editor
Heartsong Presents
PO Box 719
Uhrichsville, Ohio 44683

1. Did you enjoy reading *Sweet Harmony* by Janice Hanna?
   ❑ Very much! I would like to see more books by this author!
   ❑ Moderately. I would have enjoyed it more if

   _____

   _____

   _____

2. Are you a member of **Heartsong Presents**? ❑ Yes ❑ No
   If no, where did you purchase this book? _____

   _____

3. How would you rate, on a scale from 1 (poor) to 5 (superior), the cover design? _____

4. On a scale from 1 (poor) to 10 (superior), please rate the following elements.

   ____ Heroine   ____ Plot
   ____ Hero   ____ Inspirational theme
   ____ Setting   ____ Secondary characters

5. These characters were special because? _____
_____
_____

6. How has this book inspired your life? _____
_____
_____

7. What settings would you like to see covered in future
   Heartsong Presents books? _____
_____
_____

8. What are some inspirational themes you would like to see
   treated in future books? _____
_____
_____

9. Would you be interested in reading other **Heartsong
   Presents** titles? ❑ Yes ❑ No

10. Please check your age range:
   ❑ Under 18   ❑ 18-24
   ❑ 25-34   ❑ 35-45
   ❑ 46-55   ❑ Over 55

Name _____
Occupation _____
Address _____
City, State, Zip _____

MENU FOR
ROMANCE

Feed your craving for love-filled fiction in *Menu for Romance*, where an event planner finds herself embroiled between a flirtatious contractor and a stoic chef.

Contemporary, paperback, 320 pages, 5³⁄₁₆" x 8 "

_____